Also by Gloria DeVidas Kirchheimer

Goodbye, Evil Eye

We Were So Beloved: Autobiography of a German Jewish Community
(co-author)

Amalie in Orbit

a novel by

GLORIA DEVIDAS KIRCHHEIMER

 The Wessex Collective, 2008

ISBN-13:   978-0-9797516-3-9
ISBN-10:   0-9797516-3-2

Published by
The Wessex Collective
P.O. Box 1088
Nederland, CO 80466-1088

Web: http://www.wessexcollective.com
contact: sss@wessexcollective.com

Cover design by Gabe Kirchheimer. Photos © Gabe Kirchheimer
The Pedestrian Project © Yvette Helin

BISAC code: FIC019000 (literary fiction)

The Wessex Collective, publisher of progressive books:

If literary fiction (story telling) is the way that human beings can understand
and describe what history feels like, we believe it should be relevant to universal
and historic human experience. We believe also that literary fiction provides an
opportunity to recognize, with significant impact, the problems of societies
as well as individuals. At The Wessex Collective we are publishing books that
demonstrate an empathy for human vulnerability and an understanding of how
that is important to the larger society.

For Manny

Chapter 1

When Amalie Price came home from job hunting, she found her seventeen-year-old son Charlie sitting naked in the apartment kitchen and talking on the phone.

He threw a dishtowel over his parts and waved. "…and if the weight of Mount Washington equals the mass times the velocity, there's no reason why you couldn't transport it to the moon." He covered the mouthpiece. "How did it go?"

"Sorry, Mission Control," she said, placing herself directly in front of the fan. "I didn't take off." Never mind the smooth reentry. The job counselor who interviewed her didn't appear to be any older than Charlie. He told her that some companies actually liked to hire older employees. And why not? Amalie thought. They make good office pets and don't agitate for unionization. But since when is forty "old"?

"…Yeah, my mom's looking for a regular job…What do you mean, 'What can she do?'"

Good question, she thought. I can recite the "Song of Roland" in the original eleventh-century French as well as lots of medieval love poems, all of which come in handy for my porno translations which, thank God, Charlie doesn't know about. So much for a master's in French literature. Daddy was right. I should have learned speed typing. Months of job hunting and still no job.

"Hey, look at that sky!" Charlie hung up and rushed to the window, dropping the dishtowel along the way.

"Charlie, I know it's summer, but please…"

"Oh wow, the sunset!" Because of New York's unique pollution, there were streaks of color over New Jersey. He rushed into his room and came out wearing a pair of torn denim shorts. "I'm taking the bike out. You better check the answering machine. You got a million calls about the tenant demo."

Charlie was out the door before she could tell him to take his helmet. He refused to wear it because he claimed it suffocated the hair follicles. But suppose he got hit by a taxi? Amalie never worried this much about him while Stewart was alive.

Reluctantly she listened to messages on the machine, most from nervous tenants and a couple from the Department of Housing Preservation and Development. Amalie had inherited the job of head of the building's tenants committee from Stewart. The building was slated for demolition but she was hoping that it could still be saved. Stewart had known every inch of the facade, every cherub and mythical animal, all the bearded, horned, and cowled gargoyles on the cornices. He was always looking up, pointing out, instructing. You bastard, she thought, leaving me with this mess. And no insurance, no nothing. I have to compete with twenty-one-year-old Barnard girls for jobs.

Amalie was still seething over her visit to the employment agency. The smug interviewer had shaken his head as he looked at her résumé. "You've been out of the market so long, Amalie. This is 1987. There's new technology. I see you didn't complete our application. How am I supposed to file you?"

"This reminds me of Kafka," Amalie said.

"Yes, I know the agency. They're real sticklers." He offered her a melting Tootsie Roll from a basket. "But you know, even a person like yourself has a lot to offer and might liaise well with the public." Then he had the gall to offer her some advice: "Add a touch of color when you go out for an interview. All black is too depressing."

"So is death, you punk," she said and walked out.

The last message on the answering machine was from a woman with a German accent asking that she come in for an interview the following afternoon. Oh yes, that was last week's ad in the *New York Times* for an "Energetic creative admin. asst., self-starter, foreign lang. a + Glamorous environment, prestigious microform pub." Translation: abysmal pay, duties ill-defined.

Beware of ads that use the words "glamorous" and "creative," Amalie told herself. They lured applicants who were expected to have marketing, technical, editorial, research, financial and people skills, as well as youth, expert typing, and the ability to distinguish between regular and decaffeinated coffee.

It was almost 6:00, too late to catch anyone at the "prestigious microform pub." Amalie phoned anyway and left a message saying she'd come in for the interview the next day. What did she have to lose except time and self-respect?

In the kitchen, the papaya that Charlie bought for his fruitarian dinner was emitting its enzyme-packed effluvia, stinking up the room. He refused to refrigerate it, waiting for it to ripen naturally. (He also would not keep house plants, forswearing anything bred in captivity, though he made an exception for an ivy that was supposed to be the offspring of a cutting from a plant owned by Albert Schweitzer.) The papaya was ripening like something from a horror movie. Amalie could swear that it swelled with its own juices when left alone at night on top of an enamel counter. Fissures appeared overnight, stains oozed on the wall behind it. Still, she preferred having it here in the kitchen than in Charlie's room which Amalie regarded as the lost civilization of Atlantis. It was company of a sort, especially with Charlie out of the house. Something alive.

A freighter floated by on the Hudson which was visible from the kitchen window as a two-inch gap between buildings on Riverside Drive, two blocks away. How Stewart had loved this view. On weekend mornings, he stationed himself by the window and at 10:27 came the call: "Quick, honey, there's the Dayliner." Sometimes barges came down from Albany or oil tankers that filled the space like a hallucination.

Everything reminded Amalie of Stewart. Widowhood just seemed to get worse with time. Some of her friends considered her odd for having stayed married for so long to the same person. "You must really have worked at it," her friend Julie said, as though marriage were penal servitude. They'd been having lunch at the Pancetta cafe, off 86th Street, an unbelievably noisy restaurant where patrons were compelled to shout at each other. Julie Dryer, a muscular forty-eight and on the cusp of menopause speared an arugula leaf and declared herself full. She prided herself on her delicate eating habits as though she were a heroine in a Victorian novel in which it was vulgar for a woman to display a healthy appetite. "Consider yourself lucky," Julie said. "Now you can go out and have affairs after being mired in monogamy for eighteen years."

"Did I hear you right? Is this your idea of a silver lining?"

"Never mind. Look, you had Stewart—I said, You had Stewart as your best buddy. That's as it should be. Now it's time to move on. I'll help you."

"I appreciate it," Amalie said, loudly. But she could do with a little less nagging solicitude and Julie's tireless efforts to fix her up with dates. "I know how busy you are." Amalie put more warmth into her voice. It was amazing that Julie found the time to meet for a meal, what with her frenetic schedule as a development officer at Columbia University and her rigorous program of exercise classes which were like a religion with her. Stewart was amused by Julie but also found her expertise useful when applying for grants.

"You have to get out more," Julie said, waving away the special chocolate dessert. "One whiff of caffeine and I'm flashing like a police cruiser. Stewart would want you to go out."

"What?"

"I said, he'd want you to go out. And don't use Charlie or the tenant stuff as an excuse."

"How do you know what Stewart would want?" Amalie was annoyed.

"I know. We did spend a lot of time together that last year, may he rest in peace." Julie smiled.

"What's that mysterious smile?" Amalie asked.

"I mean professionally, idiot. You do get to know a person. Quirks, weak spots…" She trailed off. "Well, he was no goody-good."

"What are you trying to say, Julie? Your circumlocutions are exasperating."

"Circumlocutions, is it? I love that."

"Is there something you'd like to tell me just to round out the picture of my husband whom I was married to for eighteen years?" Amalie hated where her thoughts were going. "Tell me, just for the record weren't you out of town that weekend, when the accident happened?"

"Yeah, I think so. But that's not unusual for me. You know how I love to get away to the cabin." Julie had a small ramshackle place on Lake Champlain on the Vermont side. Very convenient, Amalie thought, if I really wanted to believe that something was going on between them. Julie frowned. "Why are you asking me at this late date?"

"No reason. Just trying to remember who was in town, who I called. No, it's on me." Amalie snatched the check, feeling guilty for suspecting her friend. "Let's not come back here again, OK?" I can't let myself be thinking like this, she told herself as they parted.

When the phone rang around 6:00 in the office of Warwick & Berger MicroPubs Marshall Berger and his assistant Hannelore Links had just finished having sex on Marshall's couch.

"Well, we have another prospective employee," Hannelore said with satisfaction after listening to the phone message. "But I still think we would have attracted a higher caliber if we had left in the part about meeting authors."

"No, no, and no." Marshall said tiredly. "All our authors are dead."

"But we don't want any more disasters showing up," Hannelore said. "If I had my way we would hire only Asians."

Marshall knew that what she really meant was, If I had my way we'd hire only Europeans. But she wouldn't have the nerve to say it. Maybe she was hoping they'd have a cozy dinner tonight. She was his factotum, amanuensis, slave, and right hand that often offended him. To make sure she didn't take him for granted, he decided to go home to Englewood Cliffs though nobody lived in the house any more except for him.

Hannelore smiled cheerfully. It was his prerogative. She had no rights, no rights. But let him just remember that without her, the business would collapse.

"Clean that crap off my desk, will you," he said in parting.

From the roll of toilet paper on her desk, Hannelore broke off a piece and blew her nose. She cleaned Marshall's coffee cup, straightened his papers, and then walked down the hall to Customer Service.

She opened all the drawers in the first desk, rifling through their contents, looking for telltale notes indicating that its occupant might be job hunting. Aha—an error in an invoice. She marked it with a red pen. Then a large note: SEE ME FIRST THING IN THE A.M. URGENT. H. Next, the bookkeeper's office and another note: DO NOT GIVE LISA CREDIT FOR SICK DAY LAST WEEK. SHE LOOKED PERFECTLY HEALTHY. Hannelore triple-locked her own drawers, checked the safe and watered the snake plant.

She took a taxi to her apartment which was a replica of her office—same files in triplicate, same rolodex. Every memo, every brochure in the office, had its counterpart on East 73rd Street. One could never be too careful, Hannelore thought. You never know when sabotage can strike the company.

"You calling me a slut?" the receptionist was saying into her mouthpiece the next day when Amalie walked into the office of Warwick & Berger MicroPubs, a block from the Flatiron Building. The operator seemed to have a welt on her forehead. "*My* mother? You spit on *my* mother?—Wait a sec." She plugged a cord into an orifice and announced Amalie's arrival while the box buzzed. "Warwick & Berger MicroPubs, one moment… Let me tell you something. You're an animal. Yeah…Revenge? You talk to me about revenge?" She covered the mouthpiece and yelled down the hall. "Hannelore, your two o'clock is here."

A woman in her mid-forties, a few years older than Amalie and elegantly dressed, strode purposefully down the corridor, her hand outstretched.

"Miss—sorry, Ms. Price?" The two women shook hands. Then Hannelore Links escorted Amalie down the hall. Her hair was cut short like Joan of Arc's except that it was almost white. It was hard for Amalie to tell if the color was the result of fright or a bottle. Were those spit curls pasted onto her cheekbones? Given her height the woman reminded Amalie of one those heroes in a silent Russian film who's interrupted a career as a fur trapper to come and save the people. Ms. Links was wearing a lot of leather, whereas Amalie had made the mistake of wearing a low-cut blouse because of the hot weather.

They went through a semi-open area where a gaggle of women were typing, enveloped in a cloud of cigarette smoke. There was a banner across a partition proclaiming that "Christ loves you" and a group of birthday cards, most showing large-bosomed women, affixed to a wall. "We get them from the Catholic agency," Ms. Links said, waving away the smoke. Presumably the employees, not the cards. There were about 25 people on the staff. "We are very cozy," Ms. Links said. The mail boy passed, looking like something out of *The Cabinet of Dr. Caligari*, a somnambulist's walk, greenish skin, staring eyes. Amalie caught a glimpse of some cubicles, a poster denouncing euthanasia, another advertising the Frankfurt Book Fair.

The door at the end of the corridor opened and a bearded man in a white suit extended his hand. "Marshall Berger. Just came from the American Library Association Convention at the Sheraton. You know librarians at a convention..." He chuckled. "Everyone lining up to show you their ephemera."

Amalie kept a straight face and tried not to worry about showing too much cleavage.

"Well, the Dewey system also takes in erotica," he said ushering her into his office. The Links woman followed them in. Amalie hoped this wasn't going to be one of those "Tell us about yourself" interviews.

Berger threw a bunch of brochures at her. "This is what we do. We're saving history." Spanish Civil War documents, studies of utopias, unknown Victorian novels, early photographic treatises, all on microfilm or microfiche. No need to pay royalties to anyone since the copyrights, if there ever were any, had run out, and the works were in the public domain.

This was great stuff, Amalie thought. Behind that Sigmund Freud beard there was, perhaps, a mind.

Berger swiveled around and gazed out at the airshaft. Ms. Links had not taken her eyes off him. Her lips were moving imperceptibly like those of a ventriloquist as he gave Amalie a brief history. He had first begun a small press, publishing some now famous names at the beginning of their careers. Amalie recognized a couple of winners of the National Book Award, a poet recently elected to the American Academy of Arts and Letters, a Pulitzer nominee. "I had them all," he said. "Next door we had some old journalists who thought they were still working for the WPA. Upstairs, the *Rivington Street Clarion*, a real crusader. God, those were the days." On the wall behind the desk was a newspaper photo of a younger smooth-shaven Marshall Berger being led away in manacles from a demonstration on Wall Street protesting the Vietnam War. Another picture showed him standing on the back of a truck exhorting a crowd and waving a ukulele.

This is my kind of place, Amalie was thinking. Stewart would have approved. He and I probably were at that same Wall Street demonstration.

"Do you think you could make a contribution?" Berger suddenly challenged her.

How much of a contribution can a low-level clerk make, she wanted to say. Put me into the editorial department where I belong. And get some decent air conditioning so I don't drip sweat all over your microfilm.

Before she could speak, Berger motioned to Hannelore and the two women left his office, adjourning to a conference room dominated by a massive samovar and a formal portrait of a square-jowled silver-haired man. "Mr. Warwick," Hannelore said somberly. "He has been on life support for a long time. There is no hope for him."

There were also some prints—or maybe they were not prints. "Are these original Beckmanns?" Amalie asked.

"Good for you," Miss Links chortled. "Except for our chief editor nobody in this place ever heard of him. He was German you know, but Hitler didn't like his work. Now, this position you are being considered for is extremely important." As described by Hannelore, it seemed to involve everything from manually changing zip codes on 6,000 addresses to spying on the chief editor. Then there would be operations dealing with Mark and Sip—Oh, fellow workers?—No, something about databases, MARC and CIP, ISBN's and OCLC. "They come from the Library of Congress," Hannelore said reverently as though speaking of the ten commandments. "They are the highest authority."

The receptionist was shouting to a friend in the typing pool as Hannelore and Amalie returned to the outer office. "Hey douche bag, what do you want for lunch?"

"Pay no attention," Hannelore said. "Discipline is a lost science. Good help is hard to get. Of course we are seeing other applicants. The job is a plum."

"I swear to God," the receptionist was saying as Amalie left the office, "if you sleep on rough sheets, your body ash rubs off."

Hannelore walked back to Marshall's office. Widows, she was thinking, are desirable. (Lucky that she had devised the questionnaire for applicants and included a question about marital status even though it was illegal; most people didn't know that.) Widows didn't make trouble. Grief was salutary. It made people easier to live with, like her own mother, meek as a lamb after Papa died—of humiliation, mostly—a defrocked Nazi.

"Take her," Marshall said without lifting his eyes from his papers.

"My thought exactly."

"And offer her fifty dollars more a week. She'll still be a bargain."

"Suppose she doesn't want the job."

"What are her choices? She's no chick and she has very little full-time experience. She's just heads and shoulders above everyone else out there, but—"

"—fortunately she doesn't know it," Hannelore finished.

"Precisely."

These were moments she cherished, moments of complete concordance with Marshall, better than his couch. "I'll string her along a little. I'll say we are considering several others."

"Don't be an idiot. Everyone else who applied was Neanderthal. Just don't say anything about Vermont, okay?"

Hannelore got around to phoning Amalie from home at 9:00 that night, putting off the call until she arranged her cleaning woman's schedule which was noted on a card file, one card per chore, with ruled columns for dates. "I must tell you," she said to Amalie, "that Mr. Berger made a mistake when he told you the salary. It is actually twenty-five dollars a week less, but I am sure this is secondary for a person with your attitude."

Amalie had often heard about her attitude from her father, in a similar accent. "I'd like a couple of days to think about this," she said.

"There is no time. I have a Ph.D. in literature who is waiting to hear from us but we will give you the first choice because of your situation."

"What situation are you referring to, Ms. Links?" Amalie was poised to bring in the Equal Employment Opportunity Act and any other ammunition.

"All right," the other woman giggled nervously. "Why quibble? We will increase the salary by twenty-five dollars. It will be our secret. You must not tell the other girls."

Amalie needed a job fast, given Stewart's imaginative financial records which were mostly based on wishful thinking and loans to friends, magnanimously forgiven. The one tenet of Jewish law that Stewart observed religiously was the one about giving ten percent of your income to charity, broadly defined. Now that Amalie had unraveled the finances, it was clear that freelancing as a porno translator was not going to bring in enough to support her and Charlie much longer, especially if they were going to have to move to another building. At Warwick and Berger she would have a bona fide job, with sick leave, office politics, and the ecstasy of a regular paycheck. She wouldn't have to hide her translating work from Charlie any more, a boy indoctrinated by his father to do only the kind of work you believe in.

"So it is settled, yes?" Hannelore prodded. "Good."

It was hard for Amalie to keep from dancing around the room. After months of hunting she had finally managed to land a job. No more filling out those asinine application forms: JOB OBJECTIVE: *To keep body and soul together.* SKILLS: *Bed to board.* MACHINES YOU CAN OPERATE: *VCR, electronic treadmill, processor (food and word).* EXPERIENCE: *Freelance translation of French soft-core comic strips.* And interpreting ads like "Communication Arts/Interface with People." Or, "Gal/ Guy Fri Good with words." Words of Love? Yes. Words of advice? Frequently. A little shaky on the words of wisdom. That was Stewart's department.

Amalie unfolded the French comic strip she had been working on. The captions were already loosely translated. Her job was to put them into intelligible English. It would have saved time if they sent her the French. But no, she had to deal with "The Indian sutures teach us much" and "Your corpse is ripe." It was enough to turn her off sex forever, which was fine with her. It would be a relief to never again have to make sense of "Let me join you in your tomboy" and "He collated his mouth against hers." What an irony that she'd spent years studying the medieval courtly love songs of the troubadours in which women were portrayed as unattainable love objects. All for what? French pornographic comic strips which she had translated almost with zest, as though she had an affinity with the subjects.

"Cher Monsieur," she wrote. "This will be my last bill, so kindly send me a chèque since I have found—" oh, you lecher "—a new position."

Chapter 2

"I'm the Rembrandt of the butcher business," Ralph Dobrin said. Below his hands a world of raw meat throbbed with neon light. His body itself seemed to be a showcase for the choice cuts, outrageously priced. "Magic fingers. Want to see what I can do to a membrane?" He leered at Amalie.

"No thanks." The man was a creep but she had learned to hide her revulsion. It was Saturday morning and Amalie was lingering in the shop just to take her mind off the fact that on Monday morning she would be starting her job.

Ralph was the son of Amalie's neighbor, Alex Dobrin. Since father and son could not abide one another, she served as intermediary. A resident of one of Long Island's growth communities, Ralph could not understand how anyone who was normal could live in this neighborhood. "Look at that guy. He's always pushing his nose up against my window." Ralph shook his fist at the dark face peering into the shop window, the old Greek shoemaker from next door. "The guy's shop is filthy and his machines are totally rusty."

"Well, that makes him an old-time craftsman, doesn't it?" Amalie said pleasantly.

"Oh yeah? He's got four cats. He needs them for the mice. And the mice feed on —pardon me, I don't want to be vulgar— the roaches."

"A true ecological paradise, Ralph. Look at the bright side"

"Oh—" He looked puzzled for a moment. "I get it." He beamed at her. "Like Rachel Carson."

"Exactly. Are you almost through with your dad's order?" She was eyeing the head cheese and feeling queasy.

"You're too nervous, Mrs. Price. You should learn to relax."

Sure, and you're the guy who's going to help me do it, Amalie thought.

"You know what you remind me of? One of those trembling ibises you see at the Bronx Zoo."

"Trembling? I'm as steady as a rock. And am I really that skinny?" Stewart always said she was perfect.

"I worry about my dad," Ralph Dobrin was saying. "Couple of guys were here the other day asking questions about him. Your tenant group, you know? Confidentially, I don't want him getting mixed up with shady people."

"Me? Shady?" Amalie laughed. Would that I were. Add a little spice to my life. "You're talking about me and my neighbors. We're just planning a peaceful demonstration at City Hall Plaza next month along with thousands of other people whose homes are threatened. Our committee is meeting in my apartment tomorrow." Though the neighbors were panicky about the imminent sale of the building, there was a lot of resistance to participating in the rally. Some people in the house were refusing to pay their dues to the tenants committee, let alone appear at a public demonstration.

"Thing is, I promised my mom I'd take care of him. You'll drop this off, okay?" He held up a body part. "I don't have time to leave it in his mailbox like I usually do."

Both sides of the entrance to the apartment house were buttressed by trash, courtesy of the Sanitation Department strike. Some of the windows were already painted with bloody white X's, the anonymous landlord's way of telling the tenants that the building was doomed. Stewart had foreseen it all. "They can't just knock the building down," she said. "There are laws." How naive she'd been. Now, she was, by acclamation (and by default) the head of the tenants committee. And she wasn't going to let Stewart down.

In the lobby she met Charlie who was holding a flyer and some scotch tape. "I just want to put this up," he said, showing it to her.

TENANTS UNITE. COME TO THE MEETING ON SUNDAY IN 6C. LEARN ABOUT RENT STRIKES, PASSIVE RESISTANCE, AND TAKING OVER A BUILDING.

Amalie ripped it out of his hand. "What is this?" she hissed. "Are you trying to frighten people?"

"You don't understand," Charlie said. "You want to motivate people to come to the meeting, don't you?"

"What—" she spluttered, "—what is this 'taking over a building' nonsense? This is just a tenants association meeting."

"People are not going to participate if you don't jolt them into action. You want them to be prepared. I know about these things. I was trying to help you."

"Yes, I appreciate it." How dare he talk to her as though she were an idiot. "Why didn't you check with me first?"

"You *don't* appreciate it. Any time I try to do something to help you, you get all critical." Charlie's eyes were tearing up. "I can't do anything right, can I? You have no idea what goes on in the world out there, with innocent people getting beaten up. Dad would have known what I was talking about."

"That's low," Amalie said, frostily. Yes, Dad was the hero. Charlie had a great nostalgia for the student upheavals of the sixties in which his father starred. "Tell me again what it was like," he frequently asked Stewart, as other children say, "Tell me a story." He never tired of hearing how his father defended Columbia University against the Establishment in 1968, shielding Fayerwether Hall with his body for three days and nights. At home, Amalie had waited in terror, listening to news reports and praying that her young husband hadn't been beaten or trampled by police horses. How she raged against him over the years for imbuing his son with a love of action or revolution. Living—or as Amalie called it—dying—through your children.

"You just don't want to face reality," Charlie said, crumpling the flyer and throwing it on the floor. "I could tell you all kinds of stories but you never listen. You wouldn't believe the call I got before from some kid who's been living in a box behind the freight entrance of Macy's. You've got this nice group of tenants and you're the madame president, and you'll just give in to the shitty landlord."

"I can't talk to you," Amalie said. "Wait a minute—Where are you going?"

"This conversation is over," her son said. "And maybe all other conversations too. I'm going out. Don't expect me for a while."

Don't fall for this, Amalie told herself as he went out, slamming the lobby door. Stop visualizing him lying in an alley outside a head shop in the East Village. Focus, focus…on the Housing Code, on getting a permit to demonstrate, on not wearing black any more. And getting this dripping meat up to Alex. Already it was leaving a trail of blood on the old terrazzo floor.

Alex Dobrin had had an altercation a little while earlier with the superintendent—or custodial engineer as he preferred to be known. Elisha had called Amalie Price a communist rabble-rouser for stirring up trouble among the tenants. This baboon who practically salivated whenever he saw her wasn't fit to mop the ground she walked on, Alex thought.

Waiting for the young widow to light up his apartment, Alex noted that his fever had gone down. He had calculated that for every inch of garbage rising, his fever declined by a degree. Today he read in the *Times* that the ground under New York was buckling and that a geological fault ran down Amsterdam Avenue. It was logical for the fault from the west to have moved to the West Side. Manhole covers blew off in the dead of night on Broadway, the fault of the fault in the west. Everything crazy came from there, from Los Angeles.

Alex refused to see a doctor. He suspected that his illness, manifested only in a revulsion toward poultry and a desire to laugh, was caused by space organisms brought down by the last astronaut crew and housed at Columbia University's geological institute only five blocks away. He believed that if no one else was infected it was because he offered a sympathetic environment. Charlie Price, the widow's brilliant kid, agreed and had counseled him to give up meat. Thinking of doctors, Alex shuddered. The little booths in the clinic were like those in a beauty parlor, except that in each pseudo barber chair there was a bleeding patient. For his next visit, Alex anticipated a great incision in his stomach, the insides to be removed, gift-wrapped and sent to his son the butcher. Knowing Ralph, Alex figured he would put them on special sale.

He dialed his son's number, intending to tell him to forget about the meat but heard only a recorded message informing him of weather conditions from Block Island to Cape Hatteras.

He tried dialing in three-quarter time but now the line was dead. Good, he thought. This way he'd get to see Amalie who would be delivering the order. How he missed Amalie's husband, the professor. What good talks they'd had about music.

Alex had run a second-hand music store selling instruments and transcriptions of transcriptions, mostly written by himself. Stewart had seemed so interested. Secretly Alex hoped that Stewart might write his biography. Didn't these English professors have to publish or perish? Alex was leaving nothing to the world except for a few variations on other composers' themes. "Alex the Obscure," the biography might be called.

He shaved and changed his socks. The darling girl, Amalie. How she had cheered him over the years. He wished he could console her, offer her optimism which he himself lacked. She had no idea how appealing she was. Her eyes were set far apart as though she were being pulled in two directions at once—which she often was. And that red hair like a thicket, a blaze of autumn. The first time they met, it was Mother's Day and she was wearing a Venus flytrap corsage, her personal protest against the day. A fighter in her fashion.

There she was, the Scheherazade from 6C.

"I see that my son has sent me a message." Alex took the bloodstained bag from Amalie. "Did I ever tell you my idea for a concerto based on the vein structure of a delmonico steak? Yes, good. I'm happy to see you smiling. Sit, sit. Listen, you'll appreciate this." He took the bag into the kitchen while continuing to talk. "Today's paper—it's right there on the chair—the paper has a headline about a million-dollar grant to an old army buddy of mine who became a famous sociologist. Get this—" Alex returned to the living room and showed her the article. "He figured out, after years of research, that the response to a compliment is always a smile. This is what passes for science these days."

"Sounds like my dad," Amalie said. "Let's see." Yes, Herbert Marcus had made the news again. His field was the sociology of the family but because of his eminence, he managed to engage in all kinds of peripheral studies. If Amalie didn't read about him from time to time she'd never know what he was doing.

"You mean—?" Alex took the newspaper back "—Herbert Marcus, the sociologist? He's your dad and I'm only finding this out now? We were in the war together. That's World War II, in Italy." Alex was hopping with excitement. "This is amazing. When does he visit you?"

"He doesn't. He's not that kind of relative." Amalie's father surfaced from time to time, always accompanied by a new young woman. He once conducted a study showing that men lived longer, healthier lives when they had younger partners, and Herb Marcus liked to live his sociology. Amalie hadn't seen him since Stewart's funeral.

"It's not easy to be a good parent," Alex said. "Look at me. But imagine Herbie Marcus getting a million for something anyone could have told him. Now, my son, him of the psychedelic carcass charts—you see how unkind I am—when my son was a kid he would always have an asthma attack whenever he heard a chromatic scale. When he was ten he used the inside of my balalaika to hatch some turtle eggs. But he's really a good boy. He thinks that when this building goes down I'm going to move to Fernmeadow Estates, a resort for the walking dead. Can you see me there? A place with no streets. I would rather be chewed up by the wrecker."

A curious thing was happening to Amalie while Alex was talking. Only half listening, she was watching his hands move, observed with pleasure the flaring nostrils and wavy grey-white hair dipping over one fierce eye, the dark moustache. This man knows counterpoint," she thought. What would it be like with an older man, an old friend, a friend of her father's? Suddenly aware of how she was lounging on his couch, she stood up. "Where's that response to the landlord about his request for a retroactive increase?" she asked sternly. "I need it in triplicate."

Alex smiled slyly. "If you count the syllables of the landlord's statement, especially after the part that says 'Challenge,' you have a perfect basis for an aleatoric piece of music. Listen." He struck a chord on the piano.

"I haven't got time for this, Alex. I have to prepare for tomorrow's tenant meeting." Her heart gave a lurch. This would be an important meeting, a test of her leadership. If only Charlie hadn't stormed out. She needed all the support she could get. "If you don't want to end up in Zombie Estates you'd better fill out that form and bring it to the meeting." Amalie's neighbor and deputy Rosetta had evidently failed to extract the necessary information even though her job was to compile every tenant's rent history. This was crucial since the landlord seemed to have concocted his own figures. "I know that Rosetta reminded you about this a number of times."

"Rosetta is a stone," Alex said, smirking.

Amalie snorted. That was the kind of remark Stewart might make. "I'm counting on you to be there."

"I will be there." Alex kissed her hand. The touch of his lips on her skin made her shiver. That she should be so needy, so ready, shocked her.

"Now I have certain information," Rosetta the deputy announced at the tenant meeting the next day, Sunday. "But I can't reveal it at this time."

"Why mention it?" Alex said.

Amalie was having trouble concentrating on the meeting. Charlie hadn't come home last night. They had an unspoken agreement that if he wasn't home by midnight he was staying with a friend and she was not to worry. But of course she did worry. And they hadn't parted on the friendliest terms.

"Is everyone aware," asked Miss Fanchelle, a former postal supervisor, "that touching the United States mail is a federal offense?"

"Yeah, so?" asked the brawny bartender.

Their illiterate postman, said Miss Fanchelle, had told her that soon the mail was going to be distributed by Elisha, the superintendent, and as she had mentioned, it was a federal offense to lay a hand on it. Furthermore—"

"The bills they can keep," said gouty Mr. Moran.

"My phone bill had salad dressing on the envelope," a young nursing student said. "Ranch I think it was."

There was a commotion at the door as a young man shouldered his way in. "Before we go on," Miss Fanchelle interrupted herself, "who is this stranger?"

Rosetta identified him as a student community worker from the local social services center.

"As long as he's not FBI," Alex said. "He looks like the man who rang my bell last week and asked me about the sodium nitrate I was talking about in the supermarket. Because of the bread. You know they make explosives out of that stuff."

The young man with the crew cut and glassine teeth waved to them. "I'm your liaison."

"Kyrie—? murmured Alex.

How did they know he wasn't a spy from the landlord?

"His father happens to be a doctor of forensic medicine," Rosetta said proudly.

"Could we please get down to business," Amalie said, exasperated. "We're trying to plan for the rally, remember?" She hated running these meetings. How come Stewart never had any trouble with them?

"Friends—" The student extended his hands, bitten nails

prominent, à la Billy Graham "—what I'm about is community organizing. Grass ruts." (When did roots turn into ruts? Amalie wondered.) "Tomorrow we're going over to the Sanitation Union to help them with their struggle." My God, that sounded like something Charlie might say. "We'll read from Eugene Debs and give out free beer to the workers. You people in this house are the advanced cadre—"

"What is this, the Russian Revolution?" said irate Mr. Moran. "Let the garbage people do their own dirty work. Hey, that's a good one, dirty work!"

No, this was impossible. Amalie thought she was going to scream. She had to be calm, calm, she was starting a new job tomorrow, her son had disappeared. Why should she care what happened to this crummy building?

"…With your seven rooms and two hundred dollars rent, what are you complaining about?" Rosetta was scolding polished Mrs. Konarski who looked like her Pekinese dog and was equally crotchety.

The violinist who never spoke was sitting in a corner clutching what he claimed was an Amati violin while his friend whispered into his ear.

And who was this young woman with the ironed hair who was calling for guerrilla street theater at City Hall?

"What is this, a zoo?" Frantic Mrs. Konarski was eager to return to the Eclair Cafe for her rendezvous with an aging aristocrat from the former Transylvania. Moran leaned over to her, fully aware that she was repelled by his undershirt. Was she the one who left the trash outside her apartment, he asked with a leer.

"Enough!" Amalie yelled for quiet. They were here to plan for next month's citywide demonstration and not the particular problems of this building. That would require a separate meeting. Right now she was asking for volunteers to xerox flyers, make phone calls to absentees, collect more signatures for the citywide petition to be presented to the mayor, dun people for their membership dues, help with the mail—

"Touching the mail is a crime," Miss Fanchelle cried out.

"But touching the male isn't," smirked the bartender.

"They should change the wallpaper in the lobby," someone said. "Who wants to look at shepherds every day."

"And those lamps. There are some gorgeous halogens on Canal Street."

What a hopeless job this was, Amalie thought. The building was about to be taken away from them and they were worried about the decor. It was a miracle that they'd gotten this far. There was no point in announcing the loophole she had found in the landlord's plan to proceed with the sale of the building. The local Neighborhood Preservation Program had made a loan to the landlord for the express purpose of having building violations removed, but the landlord had done nothing. Amalie had gone ahead and filed the proper papers requesting a review. She wasn't going to let the matter drop even though the landlord's managing agent had requested a meeting with her to "discuss this situation like two civilized people," which she declined to do.

Rosetta's eight-year-old, Ethan, was waving a poster: STOP ALL WARS. BOYCOTT HOMEWORK. How many of these people were actually prepared to participate in a demonstration? Some of them had already been slapped with eviction notices—all illegal—and were fearful of any kind of confrontation.

As though reading her mind Mrs. Konarski asked for the floor. The landlord was threatening to throw her out because of her dog which she'd owned for eight years.

"Mrs. Konarski," Amalie said, "I would prefer to deal with this another time. We are in the middle of a general meeting here." The woman was insistent. She began to cry. "There is no way that he can legitimately evict you," Amalie said soothingly. "The law says he has to file for eviction within 90 days of finding out about the dog and of course he has known for years that you've had the dog. Furthermore"—amazing how quiet the room had become "—you can't be evicted if you're over 62. So obviously…" Amalie wasn't going to embarrass Mrs. Konarski who was well over 70 but dressed like a woman half her age.

Mrs. Konarski drew herself up while the bartender cackled. "I am paying full price at the cinemas. I am not senior."

"Let's talk about it another time," Amalie said, "but don't worry for now."

She managed to assign some jobs and extracted a pledge from everyone to contribute to the cost of legal help, if needed. The meeting broke up after the violinist's friend, a former law school student, promised to make sure the permits for the demonstration were in order.

On her way out, Rosetta took Alex aside and said she wanted to caucus with him.

"Is that what they call it nowadays?" he said, practically shoving her out the door. He stayed behind and began to busy himself with straightening out the furniture and clearing the mess Ethan had made, while Amalie flopped on her couch and watched him. "That woman is always trying to lure me into her apartment," Alex said. "Do you think she uses octopus ink on her hair?"

Amalie ignored his question. "What is this about the FBI talking to you?" she asked, remembering that Ralph had said something about a couple of guys. She was concerned about Alex but also didn't want the unsavory taint of the FBI to affect what the tenants were trying to do.

Alex laughed. The FBI guys had intimated that Elisha was keeping a dossier on him. "I'm not surprised. My tape of the

'Star-Spangled Banner' played backwards is missing. It's part of a musical experiment but I should have known that they would consider it a desecration." He had tried to get them to listen to his harmonica piece based on rye bread one day old but clearly they had no musical aptitude. Then they wanted to know about those mysterious parcels in his mailbox, the ones that left little red puddles. They'd been tipped off by Elisha. No wonder Ralph was worried about his dad, Amalie thought.

By midnight Amalie gave up expecting Charlie to come home. This would be the second night in a row. She wandered into his room, a true ethnographic habitat worthy of the Museum of Natural History, lacking only the identifying plaques. On the floor for easy access there was clean and dirty clothing, some of it female. It could belong to any number of nubile girls in his entourage. Charlie was always advising females in distress. Like father, like son.

Stewart Price had died a year and a half ago in a car accident while driving home from an academic conference in Vermont. Amalie was almost sure the accident was the result of a moment's abstraction at the steering wheel. The police said the car was half turned around, as if Stewart had changed his mind about something. Maybe he had just seen a historic marker or an antique store, or a hitchhiker. Or even an eagle. Amalie hated the way he drove. On trips to New England he was always pointing out the Taconic Mountains on one side and the Berkshires on the other, a never-ending source of geologic wonder to him. Stewart was also the only person Amalie ever knew who could drive while reading the Sunday *Times*. But there was no newspaper found in the car. Just a woman's chiffon scarf smelling of Nuit de Rêve. Did it belong to a distressed female who had left it in the car? One of his colleagues or graduate students whose thesis needed stroking? And how would Amalie ever know?

After Stewart's death, Amalie had thrown out all the files and boxes marked "Stewart: Personal." Self-preservation in time of grief. But also she didn't want Charlie discovering something best left hidden. Stewart had kept everything: report cards from grade school ("penmanship deficient," "difficulty focusing"), playbills (performances attended with other women?), restaurant matchbooks. Now, the grief dulled, curiosity was back. There were notebooks she didn't even look into. What would she have found? Violations of their marriage? But to look at someone's personal papers is also a violation.

Best not to dwell on it now.

Under Charlie's bed, cushioned in cottony dust is a paperback of *Civil Disobedience*, plus several medicine vials, clearly labeled—truthfully, one hopes—with "Aloe," "Ginseng," "Eucalyptus." And here's a do-it-yourself acupuncture kit (unopened, thank God) showing a happy Asian male in a white coat and surrounded by flowers. A backpack with all the compartments stuffed as for a quick getaway. One shelf is an oasis of order with little transparent boxes filled with multi-colored geometric shapes, silver and gold stars, sequins and confetti, remnants of Charlie's childhood. In grade school he made collages and sold them to his relatives. There was a contest: whoever said they liked his work better than Picasso's got the prize—a big kiss.

He hasn't thrown out the empty gerbil cage, an ingenious wire mesh construction with an exercise wheel, watch tower, and an elevator run by pulleys and counterweights. Devised by Stewart, it was home to twelve gerbils, predating Charlie's antipathy for anything in captivity.

The phone rang suddenly. Charlie? No. Heavy breathing. Then, was that a woman's voice? "Don't hang up, please."

Amalie hung up. Obviously a nut. The phone rang again and she picked it up. Nothing but breathing. She hung up again and decided to keep it off the hook until morning. She'd report the call first thing tomorrow.

Now fully awake, Amalie began to think about Stewart's accident again. And about all the times he worked late. Maybe there had been a woman passenger who left the scene of the accident, though the police couldn't find any witnesses. No, he wouldn't have ridden with a lunatic, someone who would make anonymous phone calls to his wife, though it's true that he was attracted to women with unusual qualities like perfect pitch and total recall about the Yankees. He also liked women with high cheekbones, an overbite, and of course, youth. Women always flocked to Stewart. Amalie knew his type though she herself didn't conform to it.

There had surely been many women at the Vermont conference. Amalie could have gone but she hated being the appendage, the faculty wife. Still, maybe it was better than staying home, imagining, and being ashamed later of her jealousy. Oh to hell with it. How important was it anyway? She popped a sleeping pill and hoped she wouldn't have a hangover from it the next morning, her first day of work.

Chapter 3

Aside from Marshall Berger's office and Hannelore's, there were no self-contained offices at Warwick & Berger MicroPubs. Everyone worked in a partitioned space where the walls were just high enough for private activities other than conversation. Dividers were decorated according to individual occupants' tastes. Outside the comptroller's cubicle there was a poster illustrating exercises for the back and one denouncing abortion, as well as something like a shrunken head that bore an amazing resemblance to Mr. Berger himself.

Amalie was given a desk just outside of Hannelore's office. It was positioned in such a way that Hannelore would be able to see her every move. "Now that you are here," Hannelore said, laying out files, cards, and piles of microfiche, "we will be able to systematize everything."

Amalie wondered how she would ever be able to make sense out of this mess. Her mind was fuzzy from the sleeping pill and anxiety about Charlie. People kept stopping by, curious about the new employee, but Hannelore shooed them away. Finally she left Amalie alone with an assignment: the alphabetization of German names with and without umlauts and American names beginning with Mc and Mac. The company had not yet decided to computerize and so most employees were still on electric or electronic typewriters.

The chief editor stopped by and introduced himself. Ah yes, Ed Fielding, the only other person who knew the Max Beckmanns. "Welcome to the Manhattan Project," he said, extending a muscular hand. "Did you know that your predecessor was accused of stealing company secrets."

"What could possibly be secret?" Amalie asked. "I thought all your materials were in the public domain."

A tap tapping of heels was heard approaching. "Panzer Division," Fielding growled and disappeared into the editorial area. For a large man he moved very fast.

Hannelore was very displeased, yes, very displeased that Amalie had been consorting with Fielding. "There are some people you must be careful about," she said. "They are not loyal." Despite Hannelore's tyranny over the staff, Amalie noticed that she never went into the editorial area, hovering at the threshold if she had any business there, as though there were an invisible shield barring her entry.

Around noon, Hannelore stopped by Amalie's desk to remind her that she was entitled to a lunch hour. "Everybody takes lunch except me." She laughed ruefully. "I have no time. It's better this way. I don't get fat."

Amalie offered to bring her a sandwich and was astounded to see the other woman's eyes fill with tears. "How considerate." Hannelore dabbed her eyes. "There are not many kind people left in the world."

"I'll never survive this," Amalie thought at a lunch counter. She felt as if she had been working round the clock even though it had only been half a day so far. Maybe Charlie had tried to phone her and hadn't been put through. She called her house from a pay phone but got her own voice inviting her to leave a message. And she hadn't figured out how to check her messages from an outside phone, being somewhat technologically-challenged as Charlie delicately put it.

After lunch she had the misfortune to ride up alone in the wire cage elevator with Marshall Berger whom she hadn't seen in the office earlier.

"Relax," he said, shifting a toothpick from one side of his mouth to the other. "You'll do fine. I can tell about people."

Amalie smiled weakly. There were raisins stuck in her teeth so she had to be careful.

"Just don't get too comfortable at the desk," he said. "Things may change. How do you feel about the country?"

"Do you mean the United States or places with trees and grass?"

He laughed. "Never mind. Forget I said anything. Carry on."

When she returned to her desk she found Hannelore rifling through her papers. "I see we think alike," Hannelore said. "I would have done it exactly the same way." A large chain of keys swung on her chest as though she were the chatelaine of an estate.

Before resuming her tally of defective microfiche, Amalie decided to call the telephone company about the nuisance phone call last night. "The police could care less, dear," the operator said. Tracing a call was complicated unless you were a business. She outlined some steps, then added that you were better off getting an unlisted number which cost extra because they would have to leave your name out of the phone book.

Amalie laughed. "Sounds like the old joke about asking for a sundae without walnuts and the counterman says, 'I'm sorry, we're out of walnuts, you'll have to take it without peanuts....'" She looked up to find Hannelore looking reproachfully at her. On the job only half a day and already making personal calls. Well, this wasn't the last one she would make. She had people to call at the local councilman's office and then at the Department of Housing. It wasn't going to be easy to find time.

The somnambulist from the mailroom dropped a stack of publishers' brochures on Amalie's desk. "Xerox them," said a female voice from the cubicle behind Amalie. Irina, an elegant older Polish woman, came around and introduced herself as the head of inventory control. "Always xerox everything. She loves that. The more copies, the better. Some women love fur and diamonds—I myself love lace—but that one loves xeroxed copies. That's all my assistant does all day." She gestured toward a young woman who was murmuring into a phone, while collating a pile of papers with frighteningly long mother-of-pearl talons. "We have high turnovers," Irina said. "The good ones leave right away."

"So you two have met." Hannelore had materialized. "I have something to show Amalie."

On Hannelore's desk was a large book with a simulated leather binding and gold trim. "Open it. It is our history."

The book was indeed the story of the company. It contained copies of every single transaction that ever took place, including the purchase of rubber bands. Customers' letters were reproduced (but probably not the complaints), along with brochures, sales reports, invoices, and photos taken at trade fairs.

"Touch the paper."

My god, this was Hannelore's holy book, the Book of Hours of Hannelore Links.

"Acid-free vellum. From goats. It is my special project. I sent my parents their personal copy with their initials in gold on the cover. It was like a long letter to them about my life in America. It is my baby." She picked up the book and hugged it.

Maybe, Amalie thought, I'll unbend and suggest lunch some time.

The worst part of having the job is not having Stewart to talk to at the end of the day. There was always so much to discuss over dinner, even after eighteen years. Charlie's latest obsession (when he wasn't sitting there with them), news items, outrages committed by Stewart's freshman English students who never learned to spell. And while Stewart talked—he did most of the talking—the moment when Amalie slipped her foot out of her shoe and rubbed her toes up and down his calf.…"What do you have in mind?" He'd smile, fork poised. "Or will you be too sleepy later?"

"I don't know. I'm not myself today."

"Oh, how exciting."

Then she'd give him a little kick. Who needed reminders of the women who ogled him, the ones who called, the junior colleagues who needed orientation over a drink? There was a lot of teasing between them but never the direct question.

The silence now is dreadful. It is like anti-matter, anti-noise. It is like hell. Maybe her phone is dead. No. Amalie looks out the window into the courtyard. A long drop. She turns on the radio, loud rock music as though to lure Charlie home. She won't call any of his friends. She has her pride. But the worry is beginning to make her crazy. This is the longest he's ever stayed out. He might be lying in a heap on the subway tracks. Or maybe he's in the middle of a training session on passive resistance. Learning to cope with tear gas or worse. She's seen the gas mask Charlie is fashioning, though he keeps it hidden in his closet, together with the wad of flyers announcing demonstrations he is planning to attend unless there are concerts that conflict. What if he is hurt, hauled off to jail, incarcerated incommunicado? He would be less vulnerable if he cut his hair. Although he believes in living in the here and now, not to speak of the where it's at, hair is to Charlie what it was to Samson. Why couldn't Charlie be interested in normal things like other kids his age? What a curse to have a politically committed child who insists on acting according to his father's principles.

Around midnight when she's sure he's lying battered somewhere, the victim of a patriotic construction worker, Charlie comes in. "You still up?" he asks cheerfully. "How was your day among the oppressors? I hope you weren't worried. I stayed with a girl I know." And before she can ask why he didn't call her he says, "Her phone was broken." *Her phone was broken?* Isn't she living at home? Or is she one of those squatters he's so fond of who live in decrepit abandoned buildings? No, Amalie won't ask. "Did anyone come to the meeting?" he inquires.

"Wall-to-wall people. Your flyers weren't necessary."

"That's good. Tell me what your office is like."

"Tell you about it tomorrow, okay? I'm not at my most sparkling now."

"You never want to talk, you know that?" Charlie sits cross-legged on the floor by her bed. "You're my mother—don't you want to know about my life?"

Other mothers complain that their children tell them nothing. This one tells her his every thought, political and gastrointestinal. But can she say to her child, Go away, I'm not in the mood to listen to you? What is she, a Medea? Charlie used to talk to Stewart for hours. They were best friends. He misses his father more than he lets on.

"So, where were you—Christ, Charlie, what is that thing you're wearing?"

"It's a *huipil*," he says with dignity. "A hand-embroidered Guatemalan shirt." Amalie knows it means trouble. "The Indians down there wear it." The trees are hung with shreds from these shirts, left by people fleeing the government troops, he explains. Whole jungles are filled with embroidered remnants, leaving a trail for the pursuers. Charlie wants to go down there soon. He's sorry he missed the chance to go to Nicaragua to help build a hospital but he was too young.

Tonight he was selling T-shirts after the Grateful Dead concert at Madison Square Garden. He almost got busted. "But I was cool." Now she notices that he's keeping one hand tightly closed, his wrist is stiff. "What happened to your hand?"

"Some dude tried to get funny. Those are valuable T-shirts, hand-screened."

"What do you mean, 'tried to get funny'?" So he got into a fight.

"They think they're so suave because they carry a switch-blade."

"*They?* You said *a* dude."

"Yeah, dude in the collective sense. Anyway it's nothing. Just a cut and I hardly got any blood on the T-shirts."

"To hell with the T-shirts, Charlie." Her voice rises. "Show me your hand."

"What's the big deal? I told you it was nothing. The knife wasn't sharp."

Gritting her teeth, Amalie says, "You know you could die from lockjaw. You haven't seen fit to go for a tetanus booster so let me see your goddam hand."

"You're such a typical mother. You know I'm almost eighteen and I know what I'm doing."

Yeah, she knows the argument: almost old enough to vote. To be, God forbid, in the army, to marry, and to screw up. What else is he keeping from her? He and Stewart were a pair, hiding news from her—about traffic tickets and the time Charlie was caught jumping a turnstile and Stewart had to go and bail him out of the police station.

"Honey, please, a little iodine," Amalie cajoles. "A Band-Aid, something to make me happy. I'll buy one of your T-shirts."

41

"You got a deal." He unfurls his fingers.

At the end of her first week of work, Amalie was summoned to Marshall Berger's office. Now I'm in for it, she thought. Some snoop must have seen me xeroxing tenant committee materials. Or maybe somebody heard me calling Metropolitan Council on Housing. Who would report her? She also had made a number of calls to the media about the upcoming rally. "Well, when am I supposed to attend to my life?" she said aloud. Fortunately Irina wasn't in her cubicle today. Now it was possible that Hannelore knew she had stolen a roll of scotch tape and some post-it notes. Hannelore kept a strict inventory of everything. Possibly Amalie had been seen sitting at Ed Fielding's desk in the editorial office, that den of subversion. Fielding had asked for help in tracking down some obscure references to anonymous Catalan poems.

Hannelore was having a bad day. The recently hired production manager, a man who used the word "fuck" as often as grammatically feasible, had just had a fight with her and stormed out of the place.

A deep silence settled over the rest of the office, broken only by the receptionist's voice on the phone, saying, "Go ahead, take the furniture, who gives a shit." A red-eyed and disheveled Hannelore informed Amalie that the president wanted to see her. Then she sniffled and said, "I have no rights here. Everyone else is permitted to take weekends off, but not me."

"Have you tried?" Amalie asked, glad that Hannelore wasn't about to give her a hard time over a number of mistakes she'd made during the week, but maybe she was leaving that to Marshall.

"Mr. Berger will not allow me any time. If I have to make a doctor's appointment he is furious."

Hard to believe, Amalie thought, but maybe Marshall was really a bastard. Just because he had photos by Lewis Hine and Jacob Riis on his walls didn't mean that he applied his social principles to real life. Maybe he was like her father, the eminent sociologist Herbert Marcus. His concept of the role of women was completely at odds with the progressive theories he professed. Ever since she was a little girl, Amalie was taught to emulate her mother, a woman whose domain was the home and ministering to her husband, despite her college education. According to Herbert Marcus, appropriate jobs for women were in teaching or nursing, or, if it was necessary to enter the world of commerce, as assistants to male executives. He was relieved when Amalie was safely married, that she was no longer his responsibility. But he was mistaken in thinking that an adjunct assistant professor like Stewart could support the two of them. He never knew that his Wellesley-educated Fulbright scholar daughter had turned her French major into—not a meal ticket exactly, but more of a snack—by freelancing as a porno translator, since she wasn't competent to do technical translation and those were the only two kinds of translating work that paid decently. And she was never interested in teaching. Stewart was not too happy about her decision, still cherishing the notion that she could continue to work on an occasional translation for a French travel agency or the French Cultural Services. But she ignored his arguments, for once.

"I think I should return to Germany," Hannelore said now. "To an orderly society. Or join a union. Well, it doesn't matter. We are consolidating. There will be changes here."

Oh oh, that sounded ominous, Amalie thought. Last hired, first fired. Back to the snotty employment agencies, the ads calling for a "strong work ethic" (Heavy overtime, weekends and nights, no extra pay) and boasting about the "informal downtown location" (decrepit space, large insects, very young staff, no air conditioning). She wasn't a translator for nothing.

"Nothing special," Marshall said when she was in his office. "You're doing fine." He had that white suit on again. It was hard to keep from blinking. "Don't be afraid to take some initiative. The chaos here is just surface. There's an inner momentum to the work. Take your cues from Hannelore." He sounded as though he was quoting fortune cookies. "I'm going to send you out with Frank—Frank McCullough, the new production guy. He's supposed to be some kind of technical genius. He'll do all the microfilming from now on so we don't have to farm it out. And don't be intimidated by Ed Fielding. He's got credentials but he fell down somewhere along the way. Dried out now. I keep an eye on him, he's an old pal. You'll find a good support system here and a lot of emotional reciprocity."

"You mean—like—friends?" This was the first time she understood the need for the word "like" used in this way.

"Friends? That's a relative term. We're a jolly group. Take that birthday party yesterday." It was Marshall's birthday and the staff had reverently presented him with a cake decorated with sugared female genitalia. The receptionist's dress had gotten wet in the rain when she went to pick up the cake and Marshall immediately gave her a $100 bill so she could replace it.

Marshall turned his chair and gazed at a photograph on the wall, a ten-year-old girl in a textile mill. It seemed to give him inspiration and he swiveled around to face Amalie. "Try to cultivate Hannelore. There's a marvelous drive about her. She gets people to challenge their own capabilities."

Yeah, and she's always catching me off guard, Amalie thought.

Marshall urged her to speak up if ever there was something on her mind, not to be afraid. No one was perfect. "There's no hierarchy," he added. We all do our jobs. We're all peers.

Everybody's equal."

"I imagine some are more equal than others," Amalie said. The man was practically foaming at the mouth with benevolence.

Marshall looked at her keenly. "That's good. I like a woman who thinks. But more importantly I want you to have a good time. Look, I'll tell you the kind of guy I am. This isn't just a company. It's a utopian experiment in moral commerce and soon, maybe, in community living. There's going to be a change in venue." His eyes took on a slightly crazed look. Like Stewart's when he got worked up about some corporate or governmental injustice. Admirable but scary.

"I think I understand what you're trying to do," Amalie said cautiously, wondering why she was called in.

"I knew you would," he said. "We're on the same wavelength, I can tell."

"I sincerely hope so," Amalie said, maybe a little too fervently. At least she wasn't being reprimanded so she could afford to say just about anything.

As Amalie left his office, she had the distinct feeling that Marshall's eyes were boring into her back. She rather liked the sensation.

Is there a refined soul who loves Sibelius and evenings by the fire? Vigorous, DWASPM, ageless, solvent, seeks youthful Freia. Photo appreciated. Dutch treat, naturally. Box 85 NYR.

Oh please! Amalie thought. Anyone can see through that ad in the *New York Review*. Some elderly miserly slob wants a young woman to minister to his perverse needs. That desperate

I'm not, Amalie thought, even though it's Saturday night, the curse of the single woman. Horny, yes, admittedly. Even Marshall was beginning to look good.

Amalie stared at the bottle of scotch with the intensity of the breakfast eater reading a cereal box. Then she poured herself a double. Ed Fielding used to have a drinking problem. Rescued by Marshall Berger. That made both men more appealing. Too bad Fielding was married. *Stop it.* Whatever happened to fidelity? Well, what am I supposed to do, immolate myself? Amalie took a large swig. What's a peccadillo among friends? "That's the spirit," she could imagine perfidious Stewart saying. Just as she was about to take another swallow, she heard Charlie's key. Grabbing a funnel she poured the liquor back into the bottle and shoved it into the cabinet.

"Ah, my child, just in time for dinner."

"Sorry, not tonight. Going out." He had on his beaded headband and a long scarf with fringes and pompoms. A dress rehearsal for a guerilla role, wherever the action was, Latin America or the Middle East. Amalie affected unconcern. "I brought you some sprouted wheat bread," Charlie said. "It's good for you. I smell liquor."

"So you do, my dear." This time she took out the scotch and poured herself a drink. "I've heard that sprouted wheat continues to sprout when it's in your stomach, but thank you anyway. So where are you going?"

"Out. Grandpa called this afternoon. Why didn't you tell me he was in the paper the other day?"

"He was in the paper the other day. What did he say? Were you nice to him?"

"Do you really expect me to answer that?"

"Quite right. Sorry," she said. Emblazon it on my chest. Not the letter "A" though that might have done for Stewart, but rather the letters "I.S." for "I'm sorry." "What did grandpa say?"

Herb Marcus had lectured his grandson on maintaining a nonpartisan umbrella and spoke of articulation of consensus. He did not ask how Charlie was nor did he ask about his daughter. According to Charlie, he seemed to cheer up when the boy mentioned demolition, gentrification, and a citywide delegation of tenants for a City Hall demonstration. "I told him we missed him at my graduation—I know he loves words ending in i-o-n. Of course I didn't say I still had to make up a gym class to get my diploma."

Those i-o-n words represented impersonal forces, concepts Herb Marcus could grasp. Amalie had figured that out a long time ago. When Stewart was in the thick of the Columbia protests, Amalie had been careful to call the emergency meetings "intra-university convocations."

"I also told him to keep his orientation cool and he liked that. Oh, and he offered to make a contribution to the teenage hotline my friends and I are setting up at the church across the street—I told you about that."

"You did?" Amalie was baffled but Charlie went on talking.

"Round-the-clock advice on drugs, parents, housing. He gave me some good ideas for setting up a board of professionals. You know, he's totally happening in the brain."

"Yes, for a social scientist he's pretty smart." Amalie's antipathy toward sociology dated from the first and last Passover celebration her parents held, just before her mother's death. The service spoke of Moses as a society dropout and went into detail about the infrastructure of Israelite society—another plague to add to the usual ten. At that time, Herb Marcus was polishing up his course on the influence of religion on family life.

"I'm going," Charlie said. "Since you asked, there's a vigil outside of Dow Chemical."

The phone rang. "Oh hi, Evan…I know, I've just been tied up." Amalie was embarrassed. Evan Diaz, a colleague of Stewart's who was an urban historian, had been of tremendous help to Amalie in the aftermath of Stewart's death. He had sorted out legal matters and dealt with the administration at Columbia. A really good friend but she had the feeling that he was probably ready for a change in their relationship. And maybe she was too. He had been divorced for a couple of years.

"Look," he said, "I know you folks are planning a rally in three weeks. My contact at the Housing Department tells me that the mayor won't be in town that day but his staff might receive a tenant delegation, two from each zip code." Evan seemed to know a lot of people involved with city housing. "What's going on with your building?"

"Oh, thanks for the info. There's this loophole I found." Amalie described it excitedly. "I filed papers for a review."

"Where did you send them?" She told him.

"Did you get a reference number? Always very important."

"Yes, I even memorized it."

"Come on, I don't believe you."

"It's S-209831A," she said gleefully.

"Good work, lady! Now how about we make a date for dinner soon."

"Yes," she said, with conviction. He was easy to be with and attractive. She'd heard he did a mean tango. "Call me next week."

"Sorry, sweetheart," Amalie said to Charlie. "That was Evan Diaz."

"What does he want?" Charlie asked, suspicious.

"He had some useful information. Now, you said a vigil. For what?"

He looked at her pityingly. "For the environment, Mom.

Clean water. Gotta get ready."

Amalie believed in clean water but also in her son's safety. She tried to interpret, from the noises now coming from his room, what he was doing, what he was taking. "Have you got your ID?" she called. "You should always carry ID with you. Just in case."

"Mom, I've been in training. I know what to do."

"Just be careful, that's all." Amalie was remembering the dudes with switchblades. But this time it was the police she was worried about. Charlie had a pony tail. That might not sit well with New York's finest. Sometimes violence is necessary…She could have killed Stewart for instilling this in their child.

"Will you be all right?" Charlie touched her arm, concern for her in those lovely dark, long-lashed eyes that elderly women used to exclaim about when he was a baby. Recently he had told her that he was "together" now. He had found his center. She studied this child-man whose mouth resembled his father's. She couldn't remember the last time she'd kissed Stewart.

How lucky she was that Charlie was on speaking terms with her. Other mothers had given up on their kids who'd left home or were into drugs. Some were already parents. Charlie didn't seem to be in a hurry to make up that gym class. Nor had he applied to any colleges. Amalie wasn't going to pressure him. If he wanted to take some time off, that was fine. It was good to have him around.

When he left, she went into his room. The gas mask was gone from the closet. So he was expecting trouble. He could have been sitting glued to the TV for five hours like other normal seventeen-year-olds, but no, he was his father's son.

Why should she be spared? Children disappeared every day all over the world: Argentina, Lebanon, Chile. Mothers carrying placards and weeping in the squares. She had never been tested, but some day, perhaps…

49

On Charlie's windowsill there were ten open coffee cans containing twigs, upon which were fastened many cocoons. What kind of beast would emerge? She should have demanded that he clean up once in a while. How was she going to be able to assert herself in the corporate world if she couldn't even ask her kid to clean up his room?

What to do tonight? She could have suggested to Evan that they get together but she was feeling too frazzled and she seemed to have a Cyclops of a pimple in the middle of her forehead. The women friends she tried were all out. Most of Stewart's married colleagues had gradually stopped inviting her to their dinner parties. First she viewed it as a sign of exquisite sensitivity: Oh how lonely she will feel surrounded by couples. Eventually Amalie concluded that the wives were leery of having a single available female at their table especially if there was no male counterbalance. Or maybe her conversation wasn't scintillating enough.

If she went to a movie, she risked having some weirdo sit next to her, or possibly getting into a fight with people explicating the movie for their companions. Through some bureaucratic glitch Amalie was still entitled to use the Columbia University gym, which was open late on weekends. She could go and strap herself to some of those sadistic machines in the training room like her friend Julie did whenever she had a free moment. Or she could run around the track with all those galumphing Nobel Prize winners and Guggenheim Fellows who seemed to enjoy blowing their noses with their fingers. She might go for a swim in the pool. Amalie drew the line, however, at entering the sauna. It was pure masochism to incarcerate yourself in a box that made you sweat. It was good for her, the attendant often told her. It drew out the poisons. "So do leeches," Amalie said.

It was only in the last few months that Amalie had begun

to feel like rejoining society. She'd had enough talk, enough spilling of emotion. In the year and a half since Stewart died she had been in a bereavement support group, a consciousness-raising group, group therapy, a book club, and very briefly a Kabala group.

Her grief would always be with her but distraction helped. A little music, a little theater from time to time, an occasional one-night stand—why not? But that would be hard to manage because Charlie always wanted to know where she was going and with whom. But Charlie wasn't going to be living with her much longer, she was sure. Then what? She could already predict that her job at Warwick & Berger MicroPubs would settle into a dull routine with few challenges. All she'd get from it aside from the obvious would be tantalizing fantasies about the men who worked there. Her brain cells would atrophy, her newly discovered muscles as a tenant leader would wither. This was not very promising.

The local newspaper, *West Side Spirit*, listed some events for tonight:

> Free. Ankh, not Angst. Workshop for the normal neurotic. (1) Pay a visit to your body. (2) A prize for your eyes: fondling objects. (3) Falling: trust exercises.

I'm a normal neurotic, Amalie thought, remembering the days back in the 1970s when people thought there was something wrong with you if you didn't go to a therapist. Her doctor's office was in his town house and he often interrupted their sessions to run upstairs to check on a roast. There were also phone calls from his stockbroker and a man who was building a boat for him. The doctor's office was decorated in high-motel chic, with pictures of wide-eyed waifs and plaques of shriveled foliage adorning the walls. His comment that "there are actually some people who are enamored of chamber music" finally led Amalie to embrace her normal neurosis as long as she could be identified as a member of that group.

Here was something. Across the street at the Church of the Incarnation there was a free concert by the Oberlin Chamber Ensemble performing a piece based on Ouspensky's *Search for the Miraculous*. Perhaps there was something to be learned from Ouspensky.

The church's community room had been transformed for the concert. Rugs covered the walls, pillows were scattered over the floor for those who preferred them to the chairs. A cross-legged barefoot male performer waited for the audience to be seated. In front of him was a row of eleven candles—four white, four red, and three orange. The only instrument visible was a small brass gong. Perhaps this was a vocal concert. The program notes proclaimed that as audiences would soon be obsolete, the people should be free to come and go, walk about, talk, or even play "gin rheumy" if they chose.

A young woman took her place behind the young man. According to the notes she was on the Oberlin faculty and a specialist in Indian music (Ah, those sutures again!). She wore a fixed smile, either of beatitude or constipation. Somewhere in her travels she had learned that it was good to burp often and in public.

Amalie checked the audience, familiars from the neighborhood. Just as she spotted Alex Dobrin, the chief player blew out the red candles on his right and struck the gong. This must be the introduction. Alex seemed to be enjoying it. In silence the player relit the red candles and extinguished the orange ones on his left. Amalie was struggling with concepts of right and left (…left hand is the dreamer…sitting at the right hand of the Lord, etc.). With a flourish, the player whipped out a ram's horn from the folds of his raiment and blew a warbled note while his assistant continued to smile.

The gong is gonging, the assistant has sprouted finger cymbals, candles are lit and relit at a furious pace. Amalie wonders if this has something to do with the concept of music unheard being sweeter still. Stewart would surely have walked out. Maybe there's a mathematical pattern. Math was always Amalie's weakest subject. For example, if the giant sixteen-ounce size costs $2.89 on special sale, is it preferable to buy the twenty-ounce size at the regular price?

She looked at Alex. His eyes slanted down a bit. His mouth was hidden beneath the moustache. He turned and saw her. A curious, appraising stare. She lowered her eyes.

The performance finally ended when the players leapt up and shouted in unison: "Logarithm!"

She made her way over to Alex. "OK, what was that all about?"

He carefully put on his Greek fisherman's cap and thought for a moment. "Not everyone can be Bach, may he rest in peace. Try and think of the rhythms and sonorities coming from the audience itself."

"Coughing and snoring," Amalie said. "I don't buy it, even from you." She let herself be guided across the street. It was the first time a man had put his arm around her since Stewart's death. It was too comforting. "How's your moon bug?" she asked, pulling away a little.

"You're making fun of me," he said. "I don't mind. Your wonderful boy takes me seriously. I saw him go out before. He looked as though he was on his way to the Arctic."

Wearing his padded jacket in the heat of summer, probably to cushion any blows he might receive.

The elevator was out of order again so they walked up slowly. "May I propose a neighborly cup of tea?" Alex's voice shook a little. Perhaps he was winded from the climb. "Unless you have other plans…?"

Other plans. No such luck. But given her present susceptibility, it was probably best to decline the invitation. "Got some paperwork to catch up on. Some other time?" Alex seemed disappointed and relieved at the same time.

The phone was ringing when Amalie entered her apartment. Quickly she rehearsed what the operator suggested she do in case of another crank call.

"Officer Borelli, 24th precinct," said the voice. "Are you the mother of Charles Price?"

Chapter 4

"Ma'am? You there?" Officer Borelli was saying. "You have a son—"

Have, he said, not *had*. "Is he—Is he hurt?" Amalie's voice was shaking. "Where is he?"

"He's just fine," the officer said cheerfully. "We picked him up with some other kids for obstructing traffic outside the Dow Chemical building."

"Why didn't you let him call me?" she asked indignantly. "They're allowed one phone call, aren't they?" Now that she knew he was all right, she could be a little more belligerent.

Borelli explained that Charlie had tried to reach her from the precinct house a couple of hours earlier but there was no answer. Then he was transferred downtown to the courthouse. She could come to the local precinct where they would give her more information.

"Why can't you tell me more now?" she demanded. What were they hiding? This is all my fault, she was thinking. For not trying hard enough to enter Charlie's world. For dismissing his concerns, joking about them. Failing this fatherless boy who's trying so hard to be a man, one his dad would be proud of.

"Just relax, ma'am. I know how you feel. I got two kids myself, Camille and Susan, four and six."

Incipient Daughters of the Revolution I'll bet, Amalie

thought grimly after she hung up. She'd have to go to the precinct then, that cheery brick building a few blocks away, with a basketball court in the back so the cops could work off their excess fury instead of beating up on poor people and long-haired children.

Amalie put on a dowdy raincoat and kerchief so as not to attract attention. After stopping at the local precinct she planned to take the subway down to the courthouse rather than go by cab. A cab driver might get lost. Also she didn't feel like competing with evangelical sermons on the radio or hysterical sports announcements in another language. She stuffed her subway kit into her purse. One never knew what emergencies might occur. The kit contained smelling salts, water, high energy candy bars, and a plastic bag for the call of nature in case the subway stalled for a couple of hours. Some people carried harmonicas and songbooks to keep up the spirits of their fellow passengers.

It was only 10:30, plenty of people on the street. Amalie walked with downcast eyes, not from modesty but from prudence, man's best friend a reminder at every step. She passed the unfinished low-income building with its stone turtles in the front and the little door marked "perambulators," and the lonely playground already in disrepair, the sandbox with broken glass.

What if this was a trap? Suppose it wasn't the police who had called? Suppose she never found Charlie. There were cases of people locked up incommunicado for months. In America. She never believed Stewart when he told her these things. Until now.

Footsteps behind her kept pace with her own. Good thing she had a four-inch hatpin in her pocket. This street was fairly deserted. Stealthily she extracted the hatpin and whirled around.

"Don't—Help!" A man staggered back. It was Ralph Dobrin, Alex's son, dressed in civilian clothes.

"Oh, it's only you." She laughed with relief.

"Goddam!" He brushed himself off though there had been no contact. "What's a nice girl like you doing out alone on a Saturday night?" Ralph had been at his accountant's, he explained, and was heading home to Long Island. His car was parked on the street because the local garages were full tonight. He took Amalie's arm. "Of course it isn't any of my business why you're out alone. I'm glad I ran into you. I been meaning to thank you for checking up on my dad. You seem to be the only person he'll allow near him." Ralph gave her a sidelong look and pressed her arm. "It's convenient, isn't it—same building. Naturally he can't give you a really good time." As Ralph spoke the odor of licorice floated out of his mouth.

"I'm not looking for a really good time, Ralph." Amalie disengaged her arm. "I'm looking for my kid."

"Kids can take care of themselves. Maybe not the girls. You know that Hunter College girls are working as domestics in Harlem? Work-study they call it. Seriously. I read it in the *Enquirer*."

They were in front of the precinct house. Amalie didn't give a damn about what Hunter girls were doing. She started up the stairs but Ralph pulled her back.

"What are you going in there for? I didn't molest you or anything, did I?" He laughed uneasily. "You're not really going in there."

"I am as soon as you let go of my arm. For God's sake, Ralph, I told you I'm looking for Charlie."

"They're good at finding people," Ralph said and took off, dropping her arm as though it was a hot lamb chop.

Inside the police station a lieutenant presided behind a large raised desk, framed like an altar between architectural friezes that ran up the side walls. A faint smell of urine pervaded the room. It seemed like an ordinary evening, no doors clanging or prisoners shouting. But who knew what went on behind those doors marked "Community Liaison" and "Warrants and Liabilities"?

Beneath a chart labeled "Unusual Disorder Plan,. 24th Precinct," two rookies were holding a discussion: "Einstein was really a moron," one of them said.

"Except in math. You got to admit."

"But a kid who don't talk till he's five?"

At a desk, a young woman was trying to control her crying. "Did he say where he was going?" an officer asked her. "Dijus have an argument?"

Amalie leaned against the dais. Her subway kit was weighing her down. Behind the lieutenant an entire wall was filled with walkie-talkies, charging and recharging themselves, as though transmitting their energy to the man behind the desk.

"Excuse me," she said to the lieutenant, "I need to find out about the arrests—"

"—Speak up, young lady," the officer said. He was so high up on his perch that it was no wonder he couldn't hear her.

She raised her voice and tried to keep it steady. "The arrests you made outside of Dow Chemical earlier…?"

"Oh yeah." He explained that some prisoners (prisoners!) had been booked here and then were taken downtown to be arraigned. Her best bet was to go to Criminal Court on Centre Street and try to locate the group. "It might take a while."

Amalie was visualizing holding pens, billy clubs, abusive prisoners. Charlie was not big and husky. He had long hair. Oh let him be safe, she prayed. I'll make a bargain with You. Let him go and I'll send money to the Wilderness Society. I'll give up meat altogether and I'll remain celibate—easy enough now. Just keep Charlie safe.

There was a commotion near the entrance. An officer was trying to calm a distraught Ralph Dobrin. "I tell you my car's gone!" he was shouting. "What do you mean how do you know if I'm telling the truth? There—she knows me. Hey—!" He waved frantically at Amalie. "Tell them who I am."

"He's a butcher," she said, hoisting her subway kit over her shoulder.

"A lot of people do it for the insurance," one of the rookies was saying as she left the station house.

We also have our sound and light shows, Amalie was thinking on the subway ride downtown. Who needs Versailles? The lights were flickering, illuminating different images—the student desecrating a book with a highlighting pen, the man enjoying his own conversation, a window washer asleep over his pail, some leather-clad twenty-somethings, nose rings glittering. The train whined like a one-note siren. "Death and destruction," a rich contralto voice proclaimed, cutting through the whine. As the lights dimmed again, the voice rose—impossible to know where it was coming from. "Take me home," it said, "Satan is here with destruction." Maybe so, Amalie thought, patting her subway kit, but at least I've got water and a candy bar.

At the next express stop, the train slowed down, the lights came on and the speaker was revealed, a woman in a tan coat, neat scarf, modest hat, a mouth as big as her face, moving independently in every direction, emitting hisses, words, complaints.

At Times Square a large boom box blasted into the subway car, followed by a swaggering young man. If only I had the guts, Amalie thought. I'd like to walk up to him and politely ask him to turn it off. But then he might pull a gun and shoot.

Then what use would I be to Charlie?

Fingering the Victorian hatpin in her pocket, Amalie caught the boom box owner's eye. He grinned and turned up the sound, snapping his fingers. "Yo, lady. You like music? Wanna dance?" As he unwound himself from his seat the train pulled into Fourteenth Street. "Catch you later," he said and bounded out of the car.

"Pssst!" Through the peephole mandated by law, minus the little metal latch, sibilance reached Alex Dobrin with a chill. "Pssst! Open the door."

"Not yet," Alex murmured, turning over. I'm not ready, Reaper."

"Pop, it's me. Open up."

Alex sat up. "Ralph?" His son hadn't been here in months. "It's the middle of the night."

"Let me in. My car's gone."

Alex peered through the peephole. Seeing eye to eye with Ralph for the first time. He hesitated, waiting for the floodgates of fatherly love to open and admit his son.

"Come on, Pop. The next train's not for hours. I got nowhere else to go."

Nowhere else to go. A cry of help. Am I a sadist? Alex opened the door and let Ralph in.

"What a night!" Ralph threw himself into a chair. "Let me just stay till it's light. If you want to go back to sleep, be my guest. My brand-new car," he moaned.

Why was it so hard to look at him? Maybe it was those idiotic sideburns. The Beau Brummel of Bay Shore. And he wanted to lure Alex out there. No thank you. Alex preferred to spend his declining years in Manhattan, in a transient hotel if necessary, composing and continuing his search for a friendly socialist cafeteria.

"The one time I park on the street. Couldn't they just take the tape deck? Believe me, you'll be better off once you're out of here. How's your fever?"

"I don't like to bother you with my complaints." That was the wrong thing to say but Alex couldn't stop himself. Someone should teach a course on how to talk to your children. Before his retirement, Alex had offered Ralph the music store. But Ralph had wanted to follow his own star, he said. Some star. Beasts' entrails. Whatever happened to truth and beauty, the father handing on the torch?

"Listen, about this demonstration at City Hall next month. I want you to stay out of trouble, Pop. You have some very radical people in this building. Your superintendent told me."

"No doubt," Alex said. "I told him that the white bread I buy has sodium nitrite in it. He thinks I'm going to blow up City Hall."

Ralph laughed uneasily. "Come on, act your age. By the way, I ran into your friend Mrs. Price a little while ago."

"A little while ago? Where?" Alex demanded, agitated.

"Heading for the police station," Ralph said. "She was looking for her son. "I was on my way to the car—those bastards. It's probably in Mexico by now. Anyway, I wish I had such a charming neighbor." He winked at his father. "Believe me, I understand."

"Just what do you understand?" Alex asked frostily.

"I wasn't born yesterday, Pop."

"Ralph, I don't know what kind of mentality you have out there where they swap wives every weekend—"

"Hold on, now—"

"—But Mrs. Price happens to be a very kind neighbor who looked after me when I was sick and took a load off your mind." Alex could feel himself shaking with rage.

"Easy easy, I didn't mean anything. Don't get upset. It's bad for the pressure. Go back to bed. I can make you some hot milk."

Alex wasn't listening. Amalie should not be wandering around at night. "You should have accompanied her. That's what a gentleman does."

"Your friend doesn't like me. Sometimes I think I repel women." He fetched a bottle of cognac from the kitchen. "Is this the bottle I got you when you retired? It hasn't been opened. You missed some fishing trip last month. You would have enjoyed it. I can't understand why you never leave the city."

"I like the people."

"Sure, I know."

"No, you don't," Alex said sullenly. Ralph would never understand. Alex belonged here, between Central Park and the Hudson River, Scylla and Charybdis. With the homeless, the demented, the mink coats on the Sabbath and the numbers tattooed on elderly arms; with the Asians, the blacks, and Hispanics that made him a citizen of the world in one square block.

"Listen, go back to sleep," Ralph said. He plumped his father's pillow and straightened out the blanket. "I'll slip out soon." He turned off his father's lamp and loosened his shoelaces. "I saw something really funny the other day. It really got to me. This black dog was crossing against the light—you know how dumb some dogs are—he wasn't on a leash. Cars were speeding down the street and one hit him when he was halfway across. The dog ran the rest of the way on three legs, his head to one side and yowling blue murder. When he got to the curb, he lay down with his legs in the air, all twisted, still howling. He didn't sound like a dog any more. A police car drives up, the cops take a look at the dog and then they drive away. I was watching from the store.

"After a long while this sanitation truck drives up and these guys in green uniforms get out. The truck had its machinery running. They got one of those big shovels they use and scoop up the dog. I couldn't tell any more if it was still yelping, the noise from the garbage truck was so loud. The back, the disposal unit opened and you could see things going around and around in it. They shoveled the dog in and the door of the unit slid shut. And that was it. I can't get it out of my head. Pop…?"

Ralph tiptoed to the bed. He reached out hesitantly and touched his father's forehead with his fingertips then quickly withdrew them. His father had a very keen sense of smell and the odor of blood was hard to wash off.

Carved into the walls of the Criminal Court Building were slogans of a bygone age, like JUSTICE IS THE EMBODIMENT OF PROGRESS, HUMANITY AND FORBEARANCE. When Amalie served as a juror, she believed it. But now, she didn't even know what was meant by justice. It depended on who you were. Justice now meant being able to take Charlie home and making him hot cocoa.

A paddy wagon was pulling into the driveway and she ran to it. "Charlie," she called through the mesh windows, "are you in there?" A grey metal door suddenly clattered down from above, forcing her to step back and hiding the van from view.

Where to now? The lobby of the Court building was full of people leaning against the Rorschach marbleized walls or sitting on the ground (there were no benches). Signs pointed to various amenities, all closed now: restaurant, psychiatric clinic, lost and found. Amalie half expected a souvenir shop. She entered an elevator with a patrolman escorting a handcuffed teenage boy. She figured she'd start with the second floor and work her way up.

Outside a courtroom people were milling around, whispering urgently. *"He's out..."* *"not out..."* *"...won't post bail..."* *"...Riker's Island..."* Inside the room the female judge was visible behind the desk only from the nose up like a Kilroy drawing from World War II. There was an American flag encased in plastic. A distinguished looking middle-aged man was addressing the judge. "All I did was take a dose of my prescription medicine. And I'm being held like a common criminal."

"Sir," the judge said, "the ordinance prohibits drinking alcohol in a public thoroughfare unless it is discreetly enclosed in a paper bag. Especially Jack Daniels bourbon."

"But, your Honor, my doctor says that drinking in moderation is good for the heart."

Wrong room. Another courtroom. Male judge to festively-dressed woman: "What's a cute chick like you doing in a place like this?"

Defense attorney: "Your Honor, my client says a hotel has no right to keep her from renting a room by the hour, especially if men do it all the time." Behind him, a chorus of women begin to declaim the Equal Rights Amendment.

Down the hall, another room. "...charged with obstructing pedestrian traffic in front of the Dow Chemical Building." This was it. Amalie scanned the immense, badly lit area. She didn't see Charlie but wasn't that one of his friends, the kid who went down to Nicaragua to try and help the Sandinistas? He began to recite, "When a long train of abuses and usurpations evinces a design—"

"—Design!" exclaimed the judge. "Young man, you have clearly never visited Monticello, that shrine dear to all Americans."

"—It's the people's right to throw off such government."

"Sir, you are contumacious! Guard! Where's the rest of the lot?"

A door opened to admit a group of teenagers accompanied by an officer. Strangely, they were all dressed alike. Amalie saw him, Charlie. There he was. Not bloodied, not limping, but resplendent in his colors as they all were. She caught his eye, waved, tears blurring her sight. He didn't wave back. It would have embarrassed him. She blew him a kiss. His group moved forward, joined by a florid and wildly disheveled man, probably their lawyer.

The judge addressed the group but it was impossible to catch all his words. The acoustics were frightful, the air was stagnant. Echoes bounced off the walls. "In view of…*prima facie*…if *a priori*…*ipso facto*…"

Amalie was so tired. Latin began to swim around in her head. "*Cui bono…mons veneris…agnus dei*…" She bolted up and rubbed her eyes. The burly lawyer was giving everyone the V for Victory sign and Charlie was charging up the aisle "Let's get out of here," he said to Amalie and dragged her outside. It was almost two in the morning.

"Stop feeling me up," Charlie said as they walked into the apartment. "I'm all right." Amalie hadn't even realized what she was doing, patting his back, running her hand up his arm, looking for fractures, trying to detect bruises. "It was great."

His exhilaration was familiar. Like Stewart's during the big anti-Vietnam War demonstrations. While she preferred to remain on the fringes of the crowds, he always pressed ahead, into the thick of it.

"I once took you to Dow Chemical," she said, trying to keep the pride out of her voice. "You were a baby. I took the stroller and all these mothers walked around the building. The same building. Because of the napalm they were making. Dad didn't even know about it until I came home and told him."

"No way!" he said admiringly. "You never said. Did you ever get arrested?"

"Never had the privilege. And I hope it stays that way. I was half crazy with worry about you, Charlie." She wondered how she could be both furious and proud at the same time.

"I did call you, as soon as I could, but you weren't home. You're never out so late. I was the one who was worried. Where were you?"

"At a neighborhood concert," Amalie said. "Alex was there."

"Oh, so you had a date," he said accusingly.

"It wasn't a date, for heaven's sake."

"Well at least you weren't out with that guy, Evan."

"What's the matter with you, Charlie? Evan is a friend. He's helped me a lot. Look, it's late. We're both tired."

"I don't like him. He's too smooth."

"You'd find fault with any man I was in the same room with."

She was surprised to see his eyes fill with tears.

"Don't you care about Dad? It's hardly more than a year…"

"How dare you!" What did he know about her grief, the erosion of her life because of Stewart's death?

"I can't believe you're already going out with men."

I wish, she almost said. If she was going out she would have had to do it clandestinely so Charlie wouldn't find out. He was such a child. "Charlie," she said, trying to maintain some control, "first you complain endlessly that I never tell you anything and now I tell you something and get kicked in the teeth for it."

"You don't understand." He threw himself down on his bed.

She hovered in the doorway. "Well, I'm sorry I wasn't here when you called. So, did you have to pay a fine, or what? Were you trespassing?"

"Obstructing pedestrian traffic, supposedly," he said grudgingly. "It's just a misdemeanor. The lawyer, Skip Fowler, posted bail and got us out after a few hours. We were released on our own recognizance."

It sounded like Gilbert and Sullivan but she wasn't about to make a joke.

"There's a court date scheduled in a couple of weeks. We'll probably get off with a fine—but who knows. Maybe there'll be a trial and we'll be sentenced to jail."

"I doubt it," she said dryly. He loved pushing her to the limit but she wasn't going to react. This was his revenge for her night out.

"Some of my friends forgot to take ID's. They had a rough time." He sat up excitedly. "You know who was there? Spock!"

"From Star Trek?"

"No, dummy, *Doctor* Spock. He came by to wish us luck. Isn't that great?"

Of course it was great. How fitting that the great man should have appeared, in a sense following up how his charges had developed. The guru of child-rearing who always ended his chapters by reassuring you that your judgment was the one that counted in the end.

"You wouldn't be where you are today, sweetie, if not for him." Amalie wasn't quite sure what she meant but it sounded right and Charlie beamed. Whoever was responsible, Charlie had turned out to be goodness incarnate, a boy who gave away a year's allowance to a needy friend; who slept on the floor for a week so a girlfriend in distress could have the bed. A youth who believed in the harmony of the universe and the healing power of good thoughts.

"A couple of people screwed up," Charlie said, obviously eager to tell her everything. "The chanting was messed up and some people forgot to wear headbands." The whole idea was for everyone to look like everyone else to make identification of individuals difficult.

Charlie was distressed because his aesthetic sense had been violated. He wants a perfect demonstration, Amalie thought, a work of art. Oh Charlie, you will never be satisfied. I bleed for your unflinching standards of perfection. "At least you're all right and that's the most important thing."

"It's not the most important thing. Dad would have seen the point. He knew what counted."

"Yes," Amalie agreed, playing second fiddle once again. But, she swore, this would be the last time.

Chapter 5

Late Sunday morning light seeps through the windows, bypassing the white X's on the panes of the vacant apartments. Amalie is sleeping, exhausted from the night before. It was daylight when she got to bed. While she sleeps the elevator in her building suddenly halts between floors. There's new movement in the trash piles downstairs in the building.

The phone rings. "You get it, darling," Amalie murmurs, not yet fully awake. But then as it continues to ring she sits up and realizes that she's alone in the bed. A hoarse voice on the other end says, "Don't hang up. I just want to listen to you talk." She slams down the receiver. It sounds like Ralph Dobrin. Maybe he's pissed at her for not helping him out at the police station last night. Or it could be that being in this neighborhood has made him a little crazy. Amalie has heard Ralph tell his customers that voodoo is rampant on the West Side. Hadn't they found chickens with their necks wrung at the 96th Street transverse in Central Park? Of course Ralph has a vested interest in poultry.

She turns on a faucet and brown water spews out, then stops altogether. "Time runneth out," she says aloud. "Am I fighting a losing battle, trying to save this building?"

She smiles. Prior to Stewart's death she never talked to herself except in her head.

Trying the water again—a thin grudging trickle—she reflects somberly that the landlord and the developer seem to have reached an agreement, despite the landlord's blatant violations of the law. It will be harder than ever to convince her neighbors to participate in a citywide rally if they believe their own building is doomed. It's for principle, for solidarity with tenants everywhere, she said in the reminder she slipped under their doors. All her work will have been for nothing if they don't at least take a stand in public.

If the building goes, everyone will have to move. Rents in the area are skyrocketing. She and Charlie will have to leave the neighborhood. Another upheaval for Amalie, another new beginning on top of adjusting to widowhood and a new nine-to-five job.

Her neighbor Mrs. Konarski, and her Pekinese, will have to go elsewhere to drop names. Elisha will no longer have the pleasure of noting suspicious return addresses like OXFAM and Grey Panthers. And Alex Dobrin, that sweet man, what will happen to him?

Amalie puts on an old robe of Stewart's which, despite many washings, retains something of Stewart. Or maybe it's her own skin that retains his imprint. She goes into Charlie's room. She needs to check his breathing as she used to when he was an infant. His black shades are pulled down as far as they can go but she can discern Charlie in his clothes, snuggled into a sleeping bag on the floor, even though the normal complement of sheets and blankets is on his bed. There's something odd about the room: small movements as though the paint is flaking rapidly. As far as she can tell in the dim light, the activity seems to be concentrated on Charlie's windowsill and dresser where the coffee cans with the cocoons are lined up. Cocoons, of course, contain something. But perhaps no longer.

Amalie slides a flashlight out of Charlie's backpack and

shines the light on a twig. She jumps back. Jesus, they've hatched! There are hundreds, maybe thousands of tiny creatures crawling around, some still emerging from the cocoons. They are about half an inch long, but with proper feeding…Amalie resists the impulse to smack the creatures with a rolled up *Village Voice* or spray them with bug killer. Her son is mad. These things are crawling all over his dresser, finding no food, except for thought, in his leaflets.

"Charlie." She shakes him. "Wake up."

He sits up, eyes closed.

"They hatched. Do something."

"*Que ora es?*"

"Those things—they're alive."

Eyes wide open. "The praying mantises hatched? Far fucking out."

"*Do something.*"

"I have to feed them." Charlie jumps out of bed. "Look at them—look at this guy. Oh God, they're beautiful. They grow real fast. Is there chopped meat in the house?"

Through gritted teeth, Amalie says, "May I remind you that this happens to be a vegetarian household, thanks to you. Now, I do not—repeat, do not wish to see a single one of those insects anywhere in this house."

"It may interest you to know that farmers pay money for them."

"Are you planning to supplement your allowance? Look, I don't care how useful or how beautiful they are." Amalie draws Stewart's robe around her and stalks out of his room, slamming the door.

He opens the door. "This happens to be my house too."

"No, you live here. I pay the rent." The bottom line. She never imagined she'd stoop so low. "We observe certain minimal hygienic standards in this apartment. If you don't like them, you're free to leave." As soon as the words are out she regrets them. *Never, never reject your child* has been graven in her mind since infancy, usually in the form of an academic lecture. Now she has scarred her son for life. Add another five years to his analysis. Suppose he takes her literally and decides to leave? "What I mean, Charlie—" giving in as usual. Motherhood is a totally impossible occupation. But now he's slammed the door.

Amalie loosens the belt of the mangy robe. Don't stifle me, Stewart, she thinks, knowing he would handle this differently. And she would have let him. She would have deferred as she so often did. Stewart made all the important decisions. He even wanted to be consulted in the matter of buying household items. The damn can opener! They almost had a screaming fight over the one she brought home without checking with him first. But she'd been so happy as Stewart's wife. Loved, coddled, protected. Stewart saying, "I'll take care of it" and "Leave it to me." Music to her ears, the harmony of the universe as Charlie would say. Avoiding argument if possible, peace at any price. If she had doubts about their bank accounts or insurances or spending for vacations, all she had to hear were Stewart's magic words: "That's my job...don't worry about a thing."

How could I be so—*quiescent*? Amalie asks herself. Charlie wasn't the only one who sat at Stewart's feet. But the truth is that if you do sit at someone's feet, you're liable to be stepped on. She is suddenly frightened at what she sees. Was she ever truly a whole person or just an outline, waiting to be filled out by the man she married? The image repels her. She needs to get away from it, away from herself.

She presses her forehead to the grimy kitchen window through which, a few weeks earlier, she caught a glimpse of a masturbating man. Demolish the building, she thinks. It isn't worth saving. The wrecker will arrive and the site will morph into a red brick co-op with a health club on the roof and faux palms in the lobby. But who cares? If cancer doesn't get me, someone in Washington will, just by pushing a button. And if that happens, I won't be able to protect my kid.

I should have been driving the car, not Stewart. Then he could have been the one to worry now. And maybe I would have given him something to worry about, like a man's denim shirt in the front seat. So what about that chiffon scarf, Stewart? I thought you were allergic to perfume. *Oh you bastard.* Amalie begins to cry. Didn't we have a pact about other people? No, we agreed it wasn't necessary. The only condition we set was that we would die in each other's arms at the age of eighty. Stewart had broken their pact.

Charlie missed his father. He wouldn't miss her in the slightest. Wallow, wallow…Who do you think you are, Sylvia Plath? Are you going to set out milk for your kid as she did before ending her life? Let's try drafting a suicide note as an exercise. The thought cheers her up and she dries her eyes. "*Dear Charlie, It's not your fault.*" What else? "*Defrost the refrigerator on Thursday and call the lawyer—under 'L' in my address book.*" Amalie reads it critically. It needs more. "*P.S. I love you. But nothing seems to be working for me now.*" Including this note, she thinks, crumpling it up and aiming for the basket, which she misses.

She has an urge to get some air, talk to a friend. She dials. "Julie—? Evan? Oh my God, I meant to dial someone else. I hope I didn't wake you."

Evan is delighted. "Must be telepathy. I was just thinking about you. Are you doing anything now?"

Just contemplating jumping off the George Washington Bridge. "Actually no. Funny you should ask." She was feeling reckless. In need of diversion and—yes, comfort.

"I hate having brunch alone," Evan said. "Take a walk over.

I've got good stuff from Zabar's. No dress code."

Amalie laughed. Just what she needed. See, Julie? I'm following your advice.

Evan's apartment was one of those palatial spaces reserved for tenured faculty at Columbia, and faced Riverside Drive. She hadn't been there since his divorce. It looked as though most of the furniture had gone, along with his wife. There was loud music by Piazzola playing on the stereo. Evan greeted her wearing an impressive apron and wielding a mammoth tool more suitable for an outdoor barbecue than for spearing the smoked fish laid out on the table. "Great music isn't it?" he said. Makes you want to tango."

"Let's do it, damn it!" Amalie said boldly. She allowed herself to be encircled and held. God, that felt good.

They began a slow tango. Just as she suspected. He was a marvelous dancer. He drew her closer and began to breathe more quickly.

"I read somewhere that it's not good to tango on an empty stomach," Amalie said. This was going too fast. "Is that plain tomato juice or is there vodka in it?" She slithered out of his grasp and drank down half the glass. "Wow! You should have stopped me. I love this kind of food. Oh Evan, don't look at me like that. You did invite me for brunch."

He laughed and sat down opposite her. "For a skinny girl you can sure pack it in."

"First of all don't call me a girl..."

He smiled and began to tell her about his share in a Fire Island house and then about a trip he was contemplating to Chichen Itza. He didn't ask how she was, so she decided not to say anything about chasing after Charlie last night and all the agony she went through.

Then he surprised her by asking where she would move to when her building was demolished.

"Oh but I sent in papers to reassess the situation. Nothing's certain yet."

He laughed. "I know, you told me. But those papers have a way of disappearing in the bureaucracy. I wouldn't count on any follow-up."

"We'll see," she said stubbornly.

Her head was buzzing. It wasn't like her to drink in the middle of the day. Evan certainly looked good in that gauzy open-necked shirt.

He put on some fado music, Amalia Rodriguez, unbelievably soulful. "This is for us," he said and pulled her up.

The couch they tumbled onto was enormous, something out of a Freudian consulting room, with a heavy tapestry back and cushions. It reminded her of a couch in the office of a Viennese internist she'd seen many years earlier for a vaginal infection. He'd called her vagina, "your flower" and gave her sulfa pills.

"I still know how to do this," Amalie thought, amazed at how quickly she was out of her clothes. It was great to be looking at the Hudson River at the same time. But she wanted to get up and turn down the music and also to lower the shades just a bit. With Stewart she always had to control the environment when they made love, part of her always wondering if it was too warm or too cold in the room, too bright, too dark. She tried not to let Evan see that she was distracted. Let go, let go, she told herself. Don't think about Stewart.

She sighed and murmured and caressed this new body over her, under her, top and bottom. How different yet familiar. And how lovely. A man.

After a while she stretched and extricated herself.

"You know how long I've wanted to do this?" Evan asked, watching her dress.

Suddenly Amalie remembered the note she had written, the

suicide note. Had she picked it up after missing the wastebasket or was it still lying on the kitchen floor where Charlie might find it? No, it was against his religion to pick up something from the floor. But what if, just this once—

In a panic she seized the phone. "Sorry, Evan, I just remembered—"

The phone rang and rang at the other end. Finally a sleepy grunt.

"It's me, sweetie. Listen, did you go into the kitchen yet?"

"I'm sleeping. What time is it?"

"One-twenty pm."

"Where are you?" he asked with huge yawn.

"Uptown. Never mind. If you go into the kitchen, don't pick up anything from the floor."

"What are you talking about?"

"Nothing." A narrow escape. "Go back to sleep."

"I'm tired…Mom? Please get some chopped meat for them, for my praying mantises."

"You mean they won't eat tofu?"

"Please…"

"What was that all about?" Evan looked amused.

"You wouldn't understand. But you're sweet. Thanks for brunch." Amalie kissed him hastily.

"Hey!" He grabbed her arm. "My mother always said it wasn't polite to eat and run. When can I see you?"

"I'll call you." Amalie ran out of the apartment.

She took a taxi home, stopping first at her local supermarket. The note was where she left it and Charlie was asleep again.

Amalie smiled. Sleep my child. Little do you know where your mother has been and how she has been disporting herself.

Chapter 6

Marshall Berger feels good when he dresses in white. That Hong Kong suit has done wonders for him. His beard makes him look distinguished. Bibliographers lie down for him. The head of acquisitions at Penn State couldn't keep her hands off him. The chief of Colgate's collection development had to be thrown out of his motel room at the last convention.

White was Gandhi's color and Gandhi is Marshall's hero. White is the color of leadership and Marshall considers himself the shepherd of these sheep at the company, especially now that Warwick is at death's door. From time to time they need to be prodded gently to keep them in line. Many of them owe him something but he never reminds them. When he springs the news of the company's relocation to Vermont at Thursday's staff meeting, he can bet that many will want to follow him even though it might be a hardship for some. In six months, this office will be history. Ed already knows about it. In fact he contributed to the whole notion.

Marshall had been complaining about the burdens of being an employer. It wasn't easy to reconcile a socialist upbringing with being a boss. "So turn the place into a cooperative," Ed said. "An employee-owned company, share the wealth." He was sitting in Marshall's office, both men had their feet up on the desk. Like in the old days when they were buddies. "You're such a hot one on democracy and consensus—in theory anyway."

Marshall was insulted. "What do you mean, 'in theory'? Don't we have staff meetings? Don't I consult on decisions?"

"Sure." Ed laughed. "Would the staff prefer red or blue tiles behind the water cooler." He wasn't very vehement. Marshall knew that as long as he kept Hannelore out of the editorial office, there wouldn't be any serious trouble.

Marshall is a little afraid of Hannelore. She mustn't catch on that he's interested in Amalie. He can't afford to antagonize her to the extent that she'll leave the company, especially at this time of transition. He thinks he keeps her happy. It doesn't take much: an apartment, a car, new colored pens and fancy vinyl folders, and a good screw once a week. Hannelore is one of those women who feel sex is a duty. She lies there, closes her eyes and thinks, not of England as Queen Victoria counseled her daughter, but maybe of Kaiser Wilhelm, Victoria's cousin. "What would your father say if he knew you were sleeping with a Jew?" he likes to ask.

"I don't care. He is dead."

If this is how Hannelore wants to atone for her father's sins, Marshall thinks, it's okay with me. Her ruthlessness toward the employees sometimes alarms him. But he leaves the dirty work to her, his hands are clean. He did reject her suggestion that they install a time clock. Hannelore is better than a time clock because she doesn't break down. Her biggest complaint is that the staff has no loyalty. But for Marshall, loyalty is as nothing compared to credentials. He grew up in a household that revered achievement, with little distinction made between famous comedians and Pulitzer Prize winners.

Marshall reveres anyone with an advanced degree, like Ed. He was gratified when Ed thought his idea was brilliant—the transformation of the company into something resembling an ideal community, like Brook Farm or New Harmony. Beautiful,

Ed said. He'd write the mission statement. You had to have one. He knew the site in Vermont. Even if his wife balked, Ed assured Marshall, he would pack up and go. In fact for them a commuter marriage might work better than the present arrangement.

What a great staff I have, Marshall thought. Irina was married to a former Hungarian Freedom Fighter, the book–keeper was related to the hippie student leader who was now a Wall Street broker. He was a little worried about Frank McCullough's buying spree for new equipment but didn't want to interfere. The man supposedly knew everything there was to know about cameras and printers.

Amalie's résumé had knocked him off his feet. There was something sexy about those Greek letters, Phi Beta Kappa. They evoked Greece itself. The Aegean Sea, whitewashed houses, gauzy robes. Sinking down into a flokati rug…

Marshall loosens his tie. What is it about that Amalie? He'd like to pour his heart out to her. He doesn't really have anyone. When he and his ex-wife speak by phone, they discuss his daughter's teeth and summer camps.

It occurs to him that Amalie is the kind of woman he'd like to go camping with. It's crazy but that's what comes to mind even though he hasn't gone on a camping trip in ten years. She's the sort of woman who seems to know what you're thinking. Why is he so sure of this? She reminds him of rest, calm. And he needs them badly. An oasis. Preferably female. He's nostalgic for the time they could have spent together when they were younger. She seems to shun attention. Maybe she was in love with her husband. What a concept, he thinks. It's not true that men in their forties are after young chicks. He's always admired maturity in women, starting with his first piano teacher. He sighs. Ah, those arpeggios. But then his father walked in on them. *Molto doloroso.* The old man was probably jealous.

Marshall is hoping Amalie will relocate with the firm. She did say her building was slated for demolition.

Najeed drops something on Amalie's desk and gives her a shy smile. She is the person who does the lowliest work at the office. Iraqi, divorced, she speaks a halting English though she has a university degree. Her daughter, whom she sees twice a year, lives with her husband in Caracas. Najeed has just returned from one of her trips there. She speaks in whispers and tiptoes around the office. She is Hannelore's slave. It's not unusual to find her asleep on the couch at 8:30 on a weekday morning after a night of stuffing envelopes, unless Frank has spent the night which he has been known to do since his wife threw him out. In return for Najeed's obedience, Hannelore doles out small favors like taking her to Bergdorf's on a Saturday. Sometimes she gives Najeed her old dresses from Saks. She is the shadow in the doorway, darting out from behind a file cabinet, slipping out of the way, effacing herself. This could happen to me, Amalie thinks. My English is better, that's all. I've got to figure out my life—or "trajectory" as Daddy would say.

"Najeed's brother disappeared a few months ago," Ed says, as he passes Amalie's desk. "Because of his politics." He's noticed Amalie's interest in the other woman. "Say, why don't we have a bite together if you're free?"

Amalie is delighted at the idea and begins to get up.

"I'll meet you at the deli in twenty minutes."

Now why can't we just walk out of the office together at lunchtime, like normal people? Amalie wonders. She sweeps the papers on her desk to one side and puts her head in her hands, just as Hannelore appears next to her.

"I wish I had time to chitchat," she says. "Don't you have

the rest of the classifying to do? If you don't apply for CIP, we don't get the LC number and it all must go to MARC when the subscription expires. Then what happens to the ABI's, did you ever think of that?" Like Amalie's father who has a fondness for words ending in t-i-o-n, Hannelore is enamored of initials. And when she seizes on a project her mind seems to encompass every possible ramification, past, present, and future. She is like the people in Herman Hesse's book, *Magister Ludi*, in which there is a cosmic game, the Bead Game, an attempt to control life and all its possibilities. "We are terribly behind," she continues. "The Library of Congress is waiting for us."

"Surely they'll find something to do in the meantime," Amalie says, watching Hannelore rush down the hall as though to her rendezvous with that august institution.

This is not what I want to be doing with my life, Amalie thinks. I have to think about a better job, none of this low-level stuff. I'm smart. I know how to organize, how to delegate, I can manage people. It's common sense. Use this as useful experience, pad the résumé a little. Make a timetable. And shouldn't I be doing something to help mankind?

Amalie isn't totally impervious to Stewart's ideals. But at this rate, she's going to get old without having done anything useful. It's wrong to expect Charlie to carry on for her.

Her guilt is something she sees in very concrete visual terms, an insistent image she could paint if she knew how to paint. It's like a heavy train dragging along behind her, composed of remnants in different shapes, weights, colors. A diaphanous one for future derelictions; ragged shreds for never having suffered from war, concentration camps, poverty. A reversible silk patch with stripes for having been happily married. Stripes for self-flagellation. Then the little squares suitable for patchwork guilt: punishment for reading a book in the middle of the afternoon, or slinking into a matinee. The one sturdy piece, hound's tooth, not sharp and not very large, is lust for other men.

Ed was waiting outside the deli but steered her to the upscale Italian place nearby. "It goes on the corporate tab," he said, not that she asked. "We'll talk about the Renaissance brochure." But once they were settled into a booth he brought up Najeed. "Her brother used to own a cafe near the Deux Magots in Paris. I passed it often. Never had the courage to go in. Story of my life, the 'almosts.'" He laughs. "I almost studied with Nabokov at Cornell. I knew a friend of a friend of Maria Callas. It's what you might call a peripheral existence."

He made it sound delightful, not being at the center of things. Perhaps it was better to be on the periphery. Easier to cut loose. That's the advantage I have—used to have, Amalie corrected herself. Stewart and Charlie were always in the thick of it.

Ed was watching her closely. "Are they hazel or brown?" she asked, giving herself a kick under the table. *What are you doing, girl?*

"Good question," he said thoughtfully as though weighing the merits of two contesting theories. "My daughter asks me that every few months."

Amalie admired his aplomb. "I don't mean to pry into your life," she said. But of course she meant to do just that. Why was she so partial to middle-aged men with careworn features and worry lines that doubled as crinkles of humor? He was surely one of those men who had gotten up at 2:00 a.m. to give his child a bottle and also knew the botanical names for plants.

"Here's my daughter." The photo showed a sullen teenager with long hair and folded arms, lounging in the doorway of a country house. *Come on, Dad, get it over with.* "She's in a 'program.'" There was a drug problem, then she got in with the

Moonies. I think she's all right now." He put the picture away carefully, smiling, worry for his child in every line.

Amalie told him about Charlie and how she ended up in Criminal Court. They smiled at each other, partners in pain for their kids. "I don't know about you," he said, "but there are people—I'm one of them—who aren't touched by history until it invades their own homes."

"Has it?"

When he was a teenager, Ed said, his father lost his job as a teacher because someone thought he saw him at a Communist Party meeting. He was blacklisted and never taught again. He died without trying to clear himself. "I suppose I could try and get his file now. For the sake of posterity. We're probably all in some file."

I'm clean, Amalie thought. At least I was before I married Stewart. She'd gotten clearance before leaving for her student year abroad. But Stewart had been an enthusiastic contributor to dozens of political and humanitarian organizations. And now, with Charlie's activities, who knew what lists they were on.

They talked a little about the company, its history, its founding by John Warwick. The company's name would soon be changed to Berger MicroPubs, with the agreement of the Warwick offspring. Hannelore had seen to the printing of new stationery a month earlier when it was clear that Warwick would be out of the picture.

"It's not a bad place," Ed said. "Good for restructuring your life. Making a new version of it so to speak. Marshall's a good guy. He takes people back…"

Just how much did Ed owe him? How much of a drinking problem did he have?

"Our kids would probably like each other," Ed said. "We should arrange a match."

"A play date."

Ed laughed. "Best way to do it is forbid them to see each other. But maybe they already know each other. Vegetarian circles are small."

"Yeah, like onion rings."

"Not worthy of you," he said, clinking glasses with her. It would be nice, she thought, if Ed conceived an overwhelming passion for her. He never once mentioned his wife.

When she got back from lunch, the production manager, Frank McCullough cornered her in the conference room. "It's you and me, babe," he said. "We're off to Hyde Park tomorrow." He was going to drive them both up to the Franklin D. Roosevelt Library to look over FDR's appointment books which were scheduled for filming. Amalie was going to write the captions.

Frank was seldom in the office because he was "on location" most of the time. McCullough was a flushed, gone-to-seed athletic type who looked unshaven and sloppy. "Don't worry, doll," he said, noticing how she was looking at his stained tie. "I'll look like a TV anchor tomorrow."

I'm nobody's babe, she thought, irritated, but decided not to say anything. She had to work with the guy. Still, Ed noticed that she was disgruntled.

"What's up?" he asked when she came into his office looking for a file.

"Nothing. Where did Frank McCullough come from?" Amalie asked cautiously. "Talk about sexist venom…"

Ed laughed. "Relax. Cut him a little slack. You have to have a sense of humor about these things." Easy for him to say, Amalie thought. He wasn't being pressed against a conference table and called "babe."

"Frank plays a mean harmonica," Ed said. "After hours, when a couple of us are still around. Marshall just melts when he hears those blues. You should stick around some evening."

Sure. Like I have nothing else to do in my spare time. You think it's easy dealing with housing agencies and city officials?

Hannelore was clearly not happy to have Amalie pulled from what she considered urgent work but Marshall was the boss and it was his decision.

Amalie had been to Hyde Park years earlier and was surprised when Frank headed for the New England Turnpike.

"That's going to take you to Connecticut," she said. His response was to step on the accelerator and swerve into the fast lane.

"You let me do the driving, OK?"

The man was sweating and smoking and she was beginning to feel sick. She opened the window on her side as far as it would go.

"Hey! You're gonna muss my hair," Frank said and pushed the automatic button to close her window halfway.

"If you don't want a mess all over the front seat," she said, "I suggest we leave it down."

Grudgingly, he let her open it again.

Their appointment was for 3:00 and it was already 2:45. They were nowhere near Hyde Park.

"This is a great road," he said, tailgating the car in front. Come on, you fuck, get out of the fast lane."

The man was lunatic. Amalie was terrified. And it was getting later and later. The library at Hyde Park closed at 4:00.

"Where the hell is this place," Frank said after a while.

"I thought you knew how to get there," she said.

"You're the navigator. I'm just the driver." He pulled into a shoulder and took off his jacket which was drenched with perspiration. "You haven't been doing your job. Gimme the map."

"I'll navigate, OK?" She turned her back on him and cursed. What a fiasco this was going to be. She finally got them onto another road and after another hour and a half they arrived in Hyde Park at 4:30. The gate was locked.

"I knew it," she said. "This was all for nothing."

"Just like a female," he said. "Moan and groan, moan and groan." He set off across the grounds leaving Amalie standing at the gate. A few minutes later he returned with a guard. He'd become sober and apologetic as he explained the urgency of their visit and the need to meet with the archivist who was still in the building.

A few minutes later they were inside and it fell to her to cajole the archivist into letting them see the materials. None too happily and watching like a hawk that they did not handle the appointment books which had been removed from their glass cases, the archivist answered Amalie's questions while Frank sniffed around and took a couple of still pictures. At one point he whipped out a tape measure and held it against the display case.

On the way home he followed her directions and didn't say a word.

Chapter 7

The staff meeting was called for 3:00 on Thursday, two days after the Hyde Park trip, but Amalie would have to miss it. She had an appointment with the lawyer who was representing Charlie's group, The Dow Dozen. They wanted to follow in the footsteps of the Chicago Seven and the Gainesville Nine, Charlie explained, as though to impress upon her that he was not a maverick but rather following a hallowed American tradition. Fowler, the lawyer, wanted to "force the issue" he had said when he phoned her but Amalie didn't know what the issue was. Each parent was being seen individually.

Amalie was nervous about absenting herself from the staff meeting. She knocked on Marshall's door, ignoring Hannelore who was guarding the premises like a basilisk. "What is it, Amalie," she asked, frowning.

"Come in," Marshall called.

"I told her you were very busy," Hannelore said on her intercom.

"Not any more." Marshall had been looking out the window and wondering if the trees were turning in Corcoran Park where he used to play ball with the guys. "Ah yes," Marshall nodded knowingly when Amalie said she had an important appointment and wouldn't be able to attend the meeting. "I used to have a regular appointment three times a week. Went for five years. It wasn't easy. Helpful, though. You shouldn't be ashamed. I know some people look upon it as a stigma. Won't even put it on their medical claims."

"I'm not talking about a shrink. This concerns my son." It was none of Marshall's business of course.

"Believe me," he said, reaching over his desk and squeezing her hand, "I respect how hard it must be for you, a single mother. My daughter's living with my ex. The kid never wants to see me." He blew his nose. "About the meeting…Ever been to Vermont?"

Amalie shuddered. She never wanted to hear that word again. That's where she lost Stewart.

Marshall continued to talk, not waiting for her answer. "You'll have your chance soon. We're relocating in about half a year."

Amalie was stunned. *Relocating?* Would she have to leave the city? Did she have any choice? Maybe she'd have to quit this job and look for another one, but she'd just started here. Was she going to have to go back to those employment agencies where returning homemakers were welcome? A few months here would count for nothing. She remembered Charlie's friend asking him over the phone, "What can she do?"

"I'm wondering why I wasn't told about the move when I was hired." Amalie was trying not to show how outraged she was.

"You don't have to make any decisions right away," Marshall said, obviously choosing to ignore her distress. "In the meantime I've asked Hannelore to take you along to Washington to see the Library of Congress people. She said there'd been some confusion at their end."

Slippery guy. Holding out a business trip as an inducement. Well, it was something to look forward to. But then the prospect of having to pull up stakes and move to another state sent a shock through her. "Oh no," she said softly.

"You'll do just fine in DC," Marshall said confidently. "I'm not a bit worried. Look, let's talk some time. Away from here. Someplace quiet."

"There's always the conference room," Amalie said.

"Not quite what I had in mind." Marshall pretended to snap a rubber band at her. "We can be friends, can't we?"

"Friends is a relative term," she said, getting up. "I'm just quoting you."

"Amalie Price, I think you will go far." He smiled appreciatively.

"From your mouth to Her ears…"

She heard him guffaw as she left his office.

A Russian émigré driver who should have known east from west eventually deposited Amalie in front of a glass box whose plaza was almost completely taken up by a sculpture of a rolling pin.

"Your taxes and mine," growled the lawyer, Skip Fowler, when she commented on it as he showed her to a seat. The walls of his office were covered with newspaper articles, awards, and photos. There were fresh flowers everywhere. He must have won a great victory. Amalie's confidence—a little shaken by the smelly dog nosing around the reception area and then by Fowler's stockinged feet—was somewhat restored. "We're going to make them sweat, by God." He pounded his fist. "Want some coffee? My girl'l bring us some. Elsie!"

A woman of about seventy came in and took the order.

"OK honey, here's the strategy." For an hour Amalie listened to the attorney outline procedures and precedents. Her mind wandered. The shelves were filled with copies of books Fowler had written on the American judicial system. There was even a festschrift put together by the American Bar Association in his honor. Fowler was wearing a mangy tweed jacket with built-in air holes for the elbows. His shoes were nowhere in sight. She was trying not to let this affect her opinion of the lawyer. Stewart always used to say she was much too influenced by style ("Even the worst reactionary gets a favorable hearing from you because he can quote from Tacitus").

"If it's a question of a fine," Amalie said, interrupting his peroration, "let's just pay it."

"I told you," Fowler roared, pounding on the desk. "This is a test case. The system has to be shown up even if we go down fighting. That reminds me—hold on a minute." He swept a pile of papers to the ground. "Where the hell's that writ of *mandamus*," he muttered.

"This is my kid, Mr. Fowler." Amalie too could pound on a desk. "I'm not interested in your *mandamus*es or *certiorari*s or *res ipsa loquitur*s. We're talking *dies irae* here—I just want to keep my kid out of jail."

Fowler's jaw dropped.

"Bad dog, bad dog," Elsie was saying in the outer office.

"Are you American?" Fowler looked at Amalie beneath his shaggy brows. "Do you call yourself an American?"

Glancing out to the waiting room, Amalie said quietly, "Your dog has shat all over your carpet."

"Excellent!" Fowler rubbed his hands. "That's a good sign. It means we're going to win. He always knows just from listening to the discussion. Hey Amicus!" The dog came in, panting. "We're going to win, right? Tell the lady." Amicus barked. Outside, Elsie was cleaning up the mess.

"Relax Ms. Price." Now that he knew he was going to win, thanks to his canine oracle, Fowler was calmer. He gave her some articles to read and said that her being a widow would be to their advantage.

At home that evening, after Amalie finished briefing Charlie on her meeting with Fowler, she asked him, trying to make it appear as a casual question, "How would you feel if we moved out of the city?" She couldn't bring herself to say where. The whole idea seemed fantastic. "That's assuming you're still living at home. I mean you might elect to go to college somewhere."

A pitying smile from her son. "Life experience is much more important to me, especially now with our government all screwed up and Mickey Mouse in the White House. Haven't you been reading about the Contra hearings? Don't you know what's happening in America?"

"Funny you should ask, considering that my nationality was questioned just a short time ago. Not only do I know what is happening in America but also in other countries like the Philippines whose location on the map I fear you have never taken the trouble to find out."

"Mom..." A warning. He gripped her wrist.

"Unhand me, kiddo."

"Why," he asked, "do you always refuse to have a civilized discussion?"

"If you look up the meaning of discussion you will see that it's not a synonym for 'monologue.'" Amalie was warming up now. "Or maybe you frown on the use of a dictionary as a tool of the oppressive educational system?"

Charlie was struggling to remain calm. If he didn't let go of her wrist soon she was going to scream. "I understand," he said, finally letting go. "This is a rough time for you."

She rubbed her wrist. The kid really hurt her.

"Look, I'm sorry Mom. Charlie kiss and make it well." An exaggerated smack on her wrist. "What's this about leaving the city. Where to?"

Amalie told him about the proposed company move. To Vermont.

"Vermont is a neat state," he said excitedly. "They have no billboards. Burlington has a socialist mayor. But how can I leave the city and all my friends? And especially with the teenage hotline just starting up?" He and his friends had talked to people at the Spyder Youth Foundation and they were enthusiastic about the idea. Charlie had also left a message with the local city councilman's assistant. "What about you , Mom? You don't know anything about rural life. You can't even drive a nail into a wall."

"I'm not the issue," Amalie said, though that was a lie. "You're the one who's always talking about settling on the land and growing your own."

"Yeah." He didn't sound convinced. "Of course by then I'll be out of the house so it won't matter to me." Charlie had been talking about moving out since he was twelve. "On the other hand I might be in jail, so who knows."

"That would solve your problem, wouldn't it."

"I think we'll just be fined. That's what happens in these cases. Fowler's a great guy. He was in Selma."

Maybe, Amalie thought, Fowler could find temporary work for her as a paralegal. She'd work hard, learning on the job, doing scut work while keeping her eyes open for a better job. Maybe think about going to law school.

"Incidentally," Amalie said while sprinkling alfalfa sprouts over Charlie's salad, "who do you think put up the eye-hooks in the kitchen? And repaired the electric mixer?"

Charlie gaped at his mother.

"Yes, none other. There are books you know. How-to and self-help. With pictures. I'm also thinking about a class on automotive engineering."

He smirked. "Like: 'Making Friends with Your Combustion

Engine'? Come on. We don't have a car, so it's all theoretical. Although, if we move to Vermont…"

An inconceivable notion, Amalie thought.

"Will you come and visit me in Vermont?" Amalie asked Evan Diaz.

"What's in Vermont, besides cows and communes?"

They were having coffee at the Central Park boathouse. The night before, Hannelore had phoned all the employees of Warwick & Berger to say that John Warwick had passed away (she was sniffling as she talked) and that a service had been arranged for the following morning at the Ethical Culture Society on Central Park West which everyone was expected to attend. When Amalie found out that she would have the afternoon off after the service, she called Evan hoping he would be free. They hadn't seen each other since that one time she had gone to his apartment.

In keeping with the latest funerary practices there was a large white board in the lobby of the chapel, mounted with photos showing highlights of the man's life: a young Warwick in a US Army uniform, Warwick in nautical jacket and cap on his yacht, Warwick with a bevy of blondes at some official dinner, Warwick shaking hands with Nancy Reagan and her astrologer, Warwick raking leaves with a small child in front of a beachfront mansion in Bermuda.

Contrary to her usual habit, Amalie had opted not to wear black, not wanting to be mistaken for a relative. Still, Hannelore seated next to her in the pew pressed her hand as though in consolation. She had been crying. "He was a great man," she whispered." Warwick was a major during World War II "but he behaved impeccably." She blew her nose. "He always showed respect for the German officers like my father. They corresponded after the war. That's how I came to this job."

Who wanted to hear about good Nazi fathers? Amalie's own father, decorated in Italy as an American soldier, never talked about growing up in Germany or how he got to the United States, deflecting all of her inquiries while she was growing up until she stopped asking, good cheer being mandatory at home.

Cheer seemed to prevail at the service too, as the speaker told one amusing anecdote after another. Judging from the happy looks on his grown children's faces, Warwick must have been one real fun guy or a rotten father. There were tributes from the employees who knew him, including one from the receptionist with the raccoon eyes who spoke of "a friend" who needed an abortion but was unable to pay for it. Warwick came through she said as someone snickered and the comptroller coughed in protest. Ed Fielding stared straight ahead, arms crossed over his chest. He was probably making up anagrams, Amalie thought. She caught Marshall's eye and he winked at her. *The king is dead, long live the king.*

The clerks were sitting together, all in black. They would have liked to look at the deceased but the coffin was sealed.

This funeral was so different from Stewart's. No unseemly emotion here, no rending of clothes, no wailing. Hannelore's face was contorted from the effort at self-control. Why did they have lilies here, the most deathly flower of all? Amalie took out her handkerchief. She would not give in to mourning now, would not think of Stewart lying in the vast cemetery situated in the no-man's-land between Brooklyn and Queens. Think of something else. The tenant rally. Pray for good weather and lots of press coverage. Charlie. A hearing to determine his fate. Amalie wanted to tell Ed about it. He had a teenage daughter. He would understand. Watching him now she had the distinct impression that they were breathing in unison. What would he say if he knew she had worked as a porno translator? *Your corpse is so ripe. Round breasts like sins which I taste with my language* (what a difference a misplaced accent mark can make).

The service over, the clerks took off for Bloomingdales, the next best thing to viewing the body. Hannelore left with Marshall.

"First time I see you in something other than black," Ed said as they lingered outside of the building. "When you first came to the office I thought of one of those Victorian cutouts."

"You mean, no substance?" If that's what Ed meant, he had hit exactly on her own notion of herself, both pre- and post-Stewart, though now Amalie thought she could detect some solid areas in formation.

"You looked as though you were trying to hide."

He seemed to be wavering about asking what she was going to do now since they didn't have to return to the office.

"I'm meeting a friend," she said, to help him out of his uncertainty.

"Well, have fun," Ed said.

He could have been a little more aggressive, Amalie thought.

Now, sitting with Evan, enjoying the prospect of future trysts, she said, "I'm serious about Vermont." She explained the relocation plan to Evan.

"Oh, I didn't even know you were actually really working fulltime."

"But I told you, Evan. I know I told you. Maybe you weren't listening." It bothered her that something as important as her life as a working person was of so little significance to him. Maybe he still thought of her as a faculty wife.

"Forgive me." Evan took her hand, turned it over and kissed her wrist.

"OK. It's possible that I didn't really say much about it." As soon as she said it, she felt herself falling into that old pattern of taking blame, being in the wrong. No—she had to stop doing it—with everyone.

"If you don't want to leave the city, there are other options. I've got connections in the field. In fact I know the developer who bought your building. John Bovisi. I'm sure he could find something—"

"You never told me you knew him."

"I'm sure I did but maybe you just weren't listening…" He smiled, knowing he had scored a point.

"That's possible," she said curtly. She knew that she was apt to forget all sorts of things. Just ask Charlie. "Anyway I don't know why I haven't gotten a confirmation of the request for a review of the sale from the housing people."

"I told you. The city bureaucracy loses things all the time. I was telling John about you. He even said he'd like to meet you. He likes to maintain good relations with tenant leaders."

"Whatever for?" Amalie was beginning to feel very uncomfortable. Was it possible that Evan had mentioned to the developer the loophole she found and her request for a review of the building's sale? If so, it would be no wonder that she hadn't heard anything back.

"Since you're off for the rest of the day, how about coming back to my place? We could improve our tango." Evan was stroking her hand.

Amalie hesitated. Something was not quite right. If she had this nagging feeling about Evan then the sex would suffer. She was faced with the choice of asking him outright how much he had told the developer, which would be indiscreet to say the least, as well as a conflict of interest on his part, as she saw it—after all, he was her friend, ostensibly helping her out—or of not saying anything at all. Did she really want to know? It would be the end of the friendship. Or was it preferable not to know, as in the case of Stewart having an affair?

"Thanks, Evan. I'll take a raincheck" (maybe yes, maybe no). " I need to clear my head."

With sudden inspiration, she thought, What better place to get a perspective on your life than the George Washington Bridge, especially on a beautiful late summer day?

From the subway station in uptown Manhattan, Amalie walked to the pedestrian entrance of the George Washington Bridge.

The river breeze was salty. Not many pedestrians on the bridge today. A man wheeling a bike, a bunch of French tourists struggling with a flapping map. Amalie would wow them with her French, or better yet with a fractured translation: *Let me join you in your tomboy…*

Below, a cement barge floats serenely down river. How Stewart loved this bridge, this river. "There's the Tappan Zee Bridge," he'd say. "Look at the Palisades, the Thousand Steps. It's as beautiful as the Rhine or the Seine."

Looking down, Amalie sees the little red lighthouse at the base of the bridge where they'd gone picnicking countless times. You walked on the slippery rocks and picked the wild shallots and dandelion greens. "Who says there's no nature in New York?" Stewart liked to say.

Amalie also loves the bridge. Loves the first glimpse of it from the highway, coming down from upstate. The lights strung across it in the early evening, the beacon light atop one tower that used to go around every minute until the city decided it was a waste of energy. Every time a heavy truck goes by the cables vibrate. The bridge sways a quarter of an inch as it was designed to do. Charlie was so excited when he walked across it for the first time when he was five years old. "Now sweetheart," his parents told him, "you're going to be in two places at once. When you reach the middle you'll see the sign. Put one foot on this side of the line and the other foot here. Now you're in New York and in New Jersey at the same time."

You can smell the sea. The salt wind brings tears to Amalie's eyes but she keeps walking and reaches the midpoint. From this height you can't see the debris on the water, the oil spills, the dead fish. A cabin cruiser speeds upriver toward Yonkers, causing a sailboat to tilt dangerously. In spring there are shad poles on the New Jersey side. Stewart and she had once gone to the smokehouse right behind the Edgewater pier. They bought a shad and ate it. No one got sick.

Lowering over the cliffs of the Palisades are the new luxury high-rise condominiums. It's a long way down to the water from the bridge. Theoretically speaking, Amalie asks herself, who would miss me if I took a flying leap? Charlie would be fine. And Daddy would develop a new sociological theory for which he'd receive accolades from the National Academy of Sciences. Some old friends might think about her with regret. Who else would miss her? There was a faithful babysitter from years ago who continued to send her Christmas cards and admired her for not buying grapes when the California farm workers were trying to unionize.

There goes the excursion boat around Manhattan, right on schedule. People are waving up at Amalie from the deck. She waves vigorously with both arms. Hey, look at me! This is my bridge, my river. You're just tourists. This is all mine, she thinks. The river, the city. They're just passing through. I'm here to stay—assuming the Indian Point reactor a few miles away doesn't act up.

She looks up at the condominiums again, lording it over the smaller houses below, an in-your-face view. Those real estate developers are ruthless. To think that Evan Diaz,

Stewart's old friend consorts with such people. Maybe he's on someone's payroll for providing information on tenant groups like Amalie's. A kind of rage sweeps though her, making her breathe hard, pumping up her muscles as though preparing her for battle. The neighbors are counting on her and she doesn't want to let them down. She's going to fight for them. They're my people, she thinks, my family, my community.

If the building goes down, I'll go down with it. But first, refile that request for a review contesting the legality of the sale. And don't tell Evan. Charlie had a feeling about him. "Too smooth," he said. Out of the mouths of babes...

Chapter 8

Just off Route 103 near Bristow, Vermont there is a cemetery dominated by a mausoleum. On the other side of the road is the Biblio Haunt, a bookshop housed in a Victorian mansion. The owner prefers to live in a trailer a few yards away. He owns 1,000 acres which he has leased to Marshall Berger with the proviso that the shop remain on the site. Legend has it that the mansion is haunted.

This is a strange location for an enterprise like Berger MicroPubs. There is no industry, no commerce in the area except for a deserted electrical plant awaiting conversion to nuclear energy—a doomed prospect thanks to fierce resistance by the town that has turned it into a cause célèbre—and a quarry that produces talc. In winter, however, the area is filled with skiers who spend lavishly, renting the A-frame chalets that stand empty the rest of the year, leaving their corkscrews and boxes of pasta, and broken garbage disposals clogged with crushed beer cans.

Only residents who can trace their ancestry back to the 1600s, when Bristow was founded, are considered true Vermonters here. Native-born individuals whose parents came from neighboring states are still considered outsiders. There is a good deal of intermarrying within the poorest families, which results in stunted, knuckleheaded children with pasty faces who throw rocks at cars on the highway. Many of these families live in old cars up in the woods, protecting themselves against incursions by county officials and the sheriff by unleashing their huge dogs when necessary. Townspeople say the wild dogs up there outnumber the people.

The bookshop owner doesn't mind the dogs straying down the mountain and growling at customers outside the shop. It reinforces the legends about the place. *Rufus Crowley* (says the flyer near the cash register) *was a railroad mogul who built this mansion as a gift for his bride. The day before he was to carry her across the threshold she was found dead with her throat cut—by man or beast, no one knows. Crowley's statue can be seen across the way at the entrance to the mausoleum. Note the outstretched hand with a flower*...Etcetera.

Marshall has known the shop for years. In his halcyon days as litterateur he went out of his way to stop by and browse in the woodpanelled rooms with stained glass windows. Piles of books covered the carpeted stairs and each room was devoted to a different category. The house smelled faintly of mouse droppings and leather covers. He'll make no changes except possibly to seal up some holes so the bats don't fly in.

Recently the town defeated a resolution that would have permitted a developer to build a game farm nearby. Local residents were in favor of the plan because it would have created some much-needed jobs. Absentee house owners who came only to ski or summer near the lake opposed it because it would have attracted too many tourists. When Marshall submitted his proposal to the town officials, it was approved by a large majority. Here too jobs would be provided: for construction of a laboratory to develop and print the microfilm, and a technical and clerical staff (since Marshall has no illusions about his staff following him en masse to Vermont); housing would be built with a certain percentage of units to be set aside for lower-income residents. Because construction will take a while to be completed, Marshall plans to house his skeleton staff in a Rutland hotel that is on the verge of bankruptcy.

The relocation experts working with Marshall have suggested a trip to the new location to familiarize employees with the site. Presented as optional, the trip will weed out the faithful from the rest.

The chartered bus left Union Square early on Saturday morning bound for Bristow, Vermont. By now Hannelore was impatient for the actual move. Marshall had made Bristow sound like another Gstaad in winter. Plenty of skiing. "Special for you," he said. What greater proof could there be of his affection? He was up there at this very moment awaiting their arrival.

In her excitement Hannelore kept jumping up and strolling up and down the aisle. "Is everyone comfortable? Did you bring jackets? It gets chilly in the mountains. How wonderful to be away from the city, away from those horrid subways."

"I thought you never take the subway," Amalie said.

"Of course I don't. I hear terrible things about them. There is only one trouble with Vermont. It's hard to find good help there."

"Certainly robots are scarce," Ed said. "You might have to settle for people like us."

Did this mean that Ed was going to move with the company, Amalie wondered.

"We will not force people to move against their will." Hannelore had been attending briefing sessions with Marshall on how best to handle employees in a relocation. One session had been a psychodrama in which he observed Hannelore pretending to be an ordinary employee. Curious how her portrayals all involved greed, carelessness, and cheating.

It was hoped that seeing the new location would sway some employees who were undecided. For some it would be an opportunity to own a home for the first time, surely their fondest dream. Hannelore could already picture her new house because it looked exactly like her grandparents' home near the Black Forest. Marshall had promised to buy her a rottweiler.

In her Porsche, she would explore that fascinating American phenomenon, the shopping mall. Pictures from the chamber of commerce showed the nearest one, just off Route 4, built like an underground bunker, a familiar structure. At last Hannelore would have a real community, neighbors who would bring her preserves. She might even join a church. In the city, in her apartment, she could have a heart attack and no one would know. It could take days before someone would say, "How come we haven't seen the lady from 12B in a while?" In the country neighbors look after one another. It is the code.

Like a chaperone on a school trip, Hannelore went up and down the aisle, her babbling ignored by those reading or trying to catch up on their sleep.

"Shouldn't we be singing peace songs?" Ed asked, leaning over Amalie's shoulder from his seat behind her. "Remember those trips to Washington and Seabrook during Vietnam?"

Well, he knew how old she was anyway. "I didn't see you," she said. "I would have remembered you if I had." How easy it was to flirt, she thought, pleased with herself. "Remember how it rained non-stop at Shoreham?" she reminded Ed. "And the barbed wire in all the restricted areas?"

Just a few days earlier Amalie had been flying over the Pentagon with Hannelore on their way to the Library of Congress. She made the mistake of telling Hannelore that her last trip to Washington had been for a peace demonstration. That had set Hannelore off on the dangers of being caught without defenses. Look what happened to Germany after the war. The Russians came in and took over half the country. And in her town there had been no miraculous recovery. For Amalie, the peace marches had been like excursions, a good excuse to see the latest exhibit at the National Gallery while making it back to the demonstration in plenty of time for the rally. "What matters," Stewart would say, pointing to the helicopters overhead, "is that we're counted."

Outside the Library of Congress, Hannelore hung back. "I have never been in a library," she mumbled.

Amalie couldn't believe it. "But you know so much. All about cataloging and OCLC and RILN."

Hannelore swallowed. "It's all right. You are with me so I won't worry."

Once they were in the bibliographer's office, she regained her aplomb. A tweedy fellow with an eye patch, he began to shrink visibly into his chair as Hannelore expounded upon her grand scheme of subsuming the Library's database to the needs of Berger MicroPubs. The man's one good eye became glazed as she strewed his desk with index cards and spoke of the Anglo-American Cataloging Rules, Two. Both he and Amalie had ceased to follow Hannelore's spiel. He was looking at Amalie who was admiring the coffered ceiling. Hannelore finally stopped speaking and impounded several manuals and brochures. These would be turned over to Amalie to read, summarize, copy, and file.

"I'm not quite clear on what you're aiming for, Ms. Links," the bibliographer said.

Thinking how nice it would be to lunch by the Potomac with the gentleman, Amalie spoke up. Leaning forward so he could feel a little warmth, she summarized their project in five sentences and showed him two documents. It was an elegant presentation as his gratified smile told her.

From Hannelore there was no acknowledgment that Amalie had performed well. All she said on the return flight was that she hoped Amalie had learned something. But Amalie, quite contentedly, was mulling over the bibliographer's sotto voce invitation to return for a follow-up visit so he could show her his incunabula.

"Aren't we having fun?" Hannelore said now. The bus was going up Route 17 past shops with names like Formica Renaissance, International House of Pancakes, and Birthplace of the American Carpet, then up to the Thruway.

After the rest stop in the fetid bus terminal in Albany, they crossed the Hudson River, shrunken now to a skimpy polluted stream, into Troy. "Armpit of the Western world," Ed's assistant termed it as he macerated his cigar. And then there were cows! Barns! A U.S. government research facility! But it was clear to Hannelore that most of the people on this bus were not impressed. They would have to be replaced. No problem. Thanks to the relocation experts she had the exact figures on the number of unemployed in the Bristow area. The experts had also prepared a profile on the kinds of employees she could expect to hire there. The studies on which the profile was based had been conducted by the noted sociologist, Herbert Marcus (a name she recognized as German). She had found the tables surprisingly clear.

Amalie was watching the road signs. Wasn't this close to the spot where Stewart's accident had taken place? He was heading home from Middlebury College. The ambulance came from Bennington. Stewart had stopped in Hoosick, birthplace of Grandma Moses, and telephoned home.

"Are you cold?" Hannelore asked. "You are shaking, poor thing. Najeed, give her your extra sweater, the one from Bloomingdales." Amalie's teeth were chattering. She was dizzy. Was she going to faint? They were very close to the scene of the accident. She found herself leaning forward, taking deep breaths. "Chew on this." Hannelore handed Amalie a cracker wrapped in cellophane with the Lufthansa emblem on it. "I always carry these."

Ed sat down next to Amalie and put his arm around her shoulders. "Take it easy," he said. "It'll pass."

"I'm all right." She closed her eyes. "It's Stewart, the car…" She could smell burning rubber. A high whine in her ears. The car horn was stuck. Something was jammed against her chest, a steering wheel, a stopped heart.

"Almost there," Hannelore said. "Then you can rest." She held an ice pack against Amalie's forehead. Where she got it, Amalie couldn't imagine but she was grateful for it.

Gradually the dizziness subsided. No one here knew the details of Stewart's death. They were explaining away her malaise, attributing it to carsickness, lack of sleep. Someone even suggested pregnancy. "Honey, don't make no unnecessary motions." Lisa the clerk with spiky eyelashes trembling with concern. Ed was expertly massaging her neck.

"I'm sorry…" This was so embarrassing.

"Pack up, pack up," Hannelore called cheerfully. "We are soon there."

Amalie was full of thanks for these people, strangers, but so good. The obstacle was still in her chest, however. The heart that has ceased to beat, the despair.

Marshall was waiting on the veranda of the Stafford Hotel for the chartered bus. He felt good about giving his crew a couple of days in the country at the company's expense. Wait till they started working at the new location. There would be trees, an atrium, a fitness and meditation center, cradle-to-grave environment. But to discourage fraternization during work hours they were doing away with the conventional single entrance, the one elevator which was an invitation to intimacy and time wasting. Instead there would be a spacious lobby with many access points. You separate departments by building transparent aerial walkways so there are no cozy spots where people can hang out together. Much more efficient. Hannelore was enthusiastic. Marshall had let Hannelore work with the architect, giving her virtual carte blanche. But then he'd had second thoughts about the whole scheme. The relocation expert, knowing his man, said, "You're creating a modern version of a historic American phenomenon, the company town. Bristow is moribund right now. The building will be a symbol of new life. You'll be a pioneer."

"Captain of industry," Hannelore corrected, preferring the military title.

Amalie couldn't sleep although Hannelore in the next bed seemed to be having no difficulty.

Why did the bus have to take that route? Did she need reminders of the scenery Stewart was looking at when he crashed? She can't help thinking of him riding around the area with a woman beside him, obediently craning her neck to look at the pair of eagles soaring above the tree line, loosening that chiffon scarf and tossing it behind her. "*Stewart was no goody-good.*" Julie's words come back into her head.

The hotel room smelled like perfume. Stewart disliked perfume, Amalie remembered. He never let her wear it. But maybe she didn't know him as well as she thought. Didn't Julie talk about his quirks and weaknesses?

She sat up in bed with a sudden urge to smoke, which she had never done in her life. It was important to understand where she might have failed her husband.

Did he resent my reluctance to hear him explain his theories? she asked herself. What else did he resent? I never liked making love outdoors and he held that against me. We even tried it in Mosholu Park but he gave up after that. Maybe Miss Chiffon Scarf was not averse to doing it al fresco. We're close to nature here in Vermont. Today I might not object. With that thought in mind Amalie lay down again and fell asleep.

Earlier, soon after their arrival, the employees had been taken on a guided tour of the Biblio Haunt, future sales outlet for an expanded Berger MicroPubs. Marshall proudly pointed out the peaked roof and turrets, the leaded windows. "I hope they get rid of those dogs," Hannelore said, unnerved to see so many canines nosing around the bargain tables on the porch of the bookstore. "They should shoot them."

Inside the Biblio Haunt it was cold and smelled of mildew. Amalie found herself standing next to Marshall in an alcove. "I own it," he said, opening his arms. He meant the fifteen rooms and crannies filled with books, the stairs piled high with volumes, the decaying antimacassars covering the few ratty plush armchairs scattered around. "Americana," he pointed to a large room. "I own all of American culture. How do you like that—me, a kid from New Jersey." Old milk glass bottles rattled on the ledges as the wind blew through cracks in the windows. This is not for me, Amalie thought, her eyes watering from all the dust.

Hannelore had managed to forage around on the side of the road for wildflowers which now decorated the hotel room she and Amalie were sharing. "We make it homey even for two nights." She slapped her chin and cheeks with a medicated cream, hoping that everyone was grateful for this trip. The expense was enormous she told Amalie, but Marshall with his customary generosity wanted to do something for his people. He had visionary ideas but sometimes got carried away.

Awakening early, with the smell of perfume in her nose—
or was it the mixed bouquet emitting its fragrance—Amalie
dressed and went down to the lobby. The front door was
unlocked. Did they feel so secure here?

To her surprise there was Marshall jogging up the driveway.
When he saw her he waved happily. "Haven't done this in
years," he panted. "Not supposed to do strenuous exercise if
you're not accustomed to it."

"But you like to live dangerously, right?" She smiled.

"I do, I do." He held out his hand. "Amalie. I've been
wanting to talk."

"Now? It's 6:30 a.m."

"Amalie." He wiped his brow.

"Marshall." She laughed. Then, to cover her embarrassment
she said, "In some tribes in Senegal, you always preface a
sentence with the name of the person you're addressing."

"I love that," he said, moving toward her.

"Will you excuse me?" Amalie moved back a step. "I just
want to look around a little."

"Okay, okay." He put up his hands in surrender. "I know
I'm not very presentable right now."

"I've seen men sweat before so don't worry about it," she
said

"Look—I won't intrude on your privacy, on your
bereavement. I just sense a connection—no, strike that. Forgive
me. This air. It puts thoughts into your head. You don't know
what you've been doing for forty odd years and you suddenly
start questioning everything."

"I know what you mean." Amalie suddenly wished she
could tell Marshall about her marriage.

"There's nothing like New England," he said with a kind of
desperation in his voice. "Ideal location for us, Vermont. Near
all those colleges. You'll like it here. You could think about

going for a Ph.D., part-time. We'd help with tuition. No, what am I doing? Don't construe this as pressure. I don't want to know your decision yet. Look, it's a beautiful day. Why don't we go into the woods. Breakfast isn't for a while. You'll teach me the names of trees."

Another Mosholu Park. Here was her chance to try it out. But it was a little too soon. She was surprised to note that Marshall was blushing or maybe it was just the exertion from his run.

"Call it a midsummer night's dream," he said.

Amalie was fascinated. She wasn't the only one to be jolted by the country.

"I like the way you listen, Amalie. Though for you it may be the better part of valor. I know, I'm rambling."

She felt there was something very engaging about Marshall now. Why had she been leery of him? What was it that had struck her as ruthless? You weren't supposed to let your guard down with a boss. They had such power over you. But who wants to be on guard all the time?

"I'm keeping you. I'm sorry." There were sounds of activity inside the hotel. Marshall turned to go in, then added, "Just bear in mind that you might benefit from staying with the company. Consider it."

The boss had spoken. Of course it would be a perfect solution to Amalie's housing problem if her building was demolished. But what would happen to Charlie? Well, Charlie would be all right. He'd leave home, travel cross-country, do odd jobs and maybe even go to college eventually. For her, moving up here might be the easy way out. An undemanding job away from the rat race of city life. The only challenge would be to fight boredom. No, it wasn't enough. She'd stagnate here. Amalie was hearing the siren song of the larger corporate—or nonprofit world, in New York City, her city. She had an inkling that she might like a job where she could exercise some power—power with conscience, as Stewart might have said. A decision maker. The idea was immensely appealing. And thinking of all the decisions she'd been making lately, Amalie wondered if the tenant rally at City Hall would be a success. She had slipped reminders under her neighbors' doors. It was less than a week away. Rain or shine. Meet in the lobby, 10:00 a.m. Friday.

She had refiled the papers contesting the sale of her building, only this time she sent them to a specific official whose name she'd gotten from her city councilwoman who was sympathetic to tenant rights.

It certainly smelled good here in the country. Good not to hear sirens and step over trash. She found a path into some woods, close to the hotel. Decaying logs were sprouting enormous funguses just like those in a fairy tale. She wondered what poison ivy looked like and whether there were bears nearby. There were lots of mossy patches, just large enough for two entwined bodies.

A faint clanging from the hotel told her that breakfast was being served and she hurried back.

In the dining room Ed motioned her over to the empty seat next to him.

"You had me worried yesterday," he said.

"My husband's accident happened near here."

He squeezed her hand and poured about half a cup of maple syrup on his pancakes.

"Are you moving with the company?" she asked.

"Most probably. You?"

"Depends," though she wasn't sure on what.

"I hear they're planning to have t'ai ch'i in the parking lot every morning," Ed said.

In the afternoon, the staff took a tour of the local cheese factory, a small wooden building from which a rank odor issued.

This was purportedly the only handmade-cheese factory left in America and perhaps that was just as well. Inside, long troughs filled with bubbling curds and whey were being stirred by young workers with long poles. The owner, the former headmaster of a prestigious private school in New York that had courted Charlie, gave a lecture on the process. Hannelore sampled the curds which tasted like popcorn. "Maybe your son could get a job here," she told Amalie. The stench was overwhelming and Amalie went outside to wait. She could just see Charlie, who was lacto-averse, up to his ears in cheese.

And in the interests of cementing good relations, they were commanded to attend a fried chicken dinner at the local church where they mingled with the local gentry, their future neighbors. Some of the employees made frequent trips to the parking lot for some clandestine swigs of wine bought at the supermarket. As a result there was a lot of good feeling and major cases of heartburn during the night.

The following day, on their way home, the chartered bus passed a large white frame building with green shutters and a large veranda. The sign in front said 1759. Center for Language Training. On the lawn a blackface jockey statue was vomiting water into a fountain. There was no other sign of life. "CIA front," Ed said. He hadn't spoken much though he was sitting right next to Amalie. Marshall had remained behind for another couple of days.

Soon they would pass that spot where the accident happened.

"You'll be okay," Ed said, sensing her unease.

Up front someone had begun to sing some dirty limericks. Hannelore was in ecstasy with her crew. Her eyes were brimming with joy. Marshall in his wisdom—that old Jewish wisdom, she thought with awe—had again made a brilliant decision.

Chapter 9

A pox on birthdays, Alex Dobrin thought, on his way to Lampedusa's restaurant with his son. Again he was hearing about Fernmeadow Estates where children were not permitted within the confines of the electrified fence unless accompanied by an adult. To hear Ralph describe the community it was a veritable hotbed of culture: amateur nights, craft fairs, a lecture series on the great sitcoms of the 1950s.

"You could even do some concertizing, Pop."

Alex shuddered. It was different when he had the store. There he had given master classes in "Music and Socialism" to a packed house. Wasn't that when he had first seen his neighbor Amalie Price? He would miss her sorely if their building went down and the tenants dispersed. She was away for the weekend, some company trip, and already he missed her.

Lampedusa's had originally been the President Theater, but now a waterfall and miniature grotto decorated what used to be the lobby. Lanterns and streamers hung in perpetual celebration from the arches.

"You know," Alex told the coat check attendant, "this is where they first performed Odets' *Awake and Sing.*"

"Is there an album for it?" she asked.

"I don't think the young lady is interested." Ralph smiled uncomfortably.

"Sorry," Alex mumbled. "It was before your time."

"But I like the classics," she said sweetly. "Especially Kurt Vonnegut."

A menu the size of the *New York Post* was put in front of Alex but he waved it aside impatiently. "You're probably too young to remember, Ralph," he said, "but this is where they did some of my incidental music. I was working with Piscator. Very avant-garde. Pirandello."

"Antipasto." Ralph smiled nervously at the waiter.

Alex pointed to the accordionist who was hoisting his instrument to his shoulders. "What do you want to bet he plays 'Funiculi, Funicula'?"

A couple of barking chords, and sure enough...

"I like this place," Alex said charitably.

"Do you, Pop? I want you to have a wonderful birthday."

Poor Ralph, so eager to please. Alex resolved to make a special effort for a change.

There was a large group at another table. Several generations, tightlipped and redfaced. The kids were kicking each other under the table. A many-tiered birthday cake had just been set down in front of the patriarch.

"A guy with a machine gun is going to jump out of that cake." Ralph leaned confidentially toward his father and they both laughed. "Hey, this is real nice." he laid his hand on Alex's sleeve.

"Whatever you do," Alex said gruffly, "don't order me a cake."

"Here's what I got for you." Ralph took a small box out of his pocket.

"You shouldn't spend money on me." Alex was embarrassed. "Buy something for the kid," a sniveling, timid, running-to-fat eleven-year-old, his grandson.

"Birthdays are a tradition and we have to keep up the

traditions, if you know what I mean." Ralph lowered his voice. "They call us 'people of the book.'"

"Only the first five." Alex unwrapped the gift. A digital watch. He had to put on his glasses to read the time though he didn't have any trouble with ordinary watches.

"It's a beauty, isn't it." Ralph was fidgeting excitedly. "The strap is leather."

What was it about leather that made his son so agitated? The sheer animal smell. Alex stared, fascinated, as the seconds changed disquietingly before his eyes. It was—no mistake about it—the exact time. Never a little earlier or later. This was time out of context.

"Listen." Ralph touched something on the watch and a tinny voice said, "*The time is now one twenty-three and fifty-nine seconds…*"

"Fine, fine. Shhh. It's wonderful, thanks. Excuse me," Alex said to the voice as he sealed it into the gift box.

Throughout the meal he was imagining the numbers changing relentlessly beneath the fuchsia wrapping paper.

Ralph brought up the forthcoming tenant demonstration at City Hall. "Stay away, Pop. There could be trouble."

"Amalie Price is our leader." Alex relished the sound of her name.

"I'm just trying to protect you." Ralph poked at his tiramisu as though a microphone might be concealed in it.

The man twisting balloons into grotesque shapes came to their table but Alex waved him away. "I already got my present." He imagined the electronic voice telling him in no uncertain terms that his life was ebbing—as though he didn't already know it.

When Amalie returned home late Monday night after the

trip to Vermont she found a sprig of freesia and a note from Charlie. *Mom. I bought these to cheer you up. My friend is coming sometime tonight but I told her not to ring the bell.*

Charlie's light was on and his door open, but he was asleep on the floor in his clothes. No more coffee cans or praying mantises. He must have gathered them up and taken them to Central Park. The bed had been freshly made, the comforter turned down for his guest. Who was it tonight? The fourteen-year-old who was disowned by her parents and hitched around the country, with time off for two abortions? Or the sixteen-year-old who was forcibly institutionalized by her parents and escaped by sliding down a rope? Months earlier Charlie had warned Amalie to pretend to know nothing if someone called and asked about the girl's whereabouts. But she didn't know where the girl was and preferred it that way, so would he please stop telling her all about the girl's bourgeois parents and her specific itinerary after escaping from Rockland State?

The girls flocked to Charlie. He was his father's son. But Amalie suspected that there wasn't much sex in his life since he had read somewhere that emission of semen results in the loss of potassium.

Charlie stirred and moved his arm in a wide arc, as though demonstrating the scope of possibilities open to him. Remembering the freesia, Amalie wrote him a note. *Dear comfort of my old age. Now I believe in the harmony of the universe. I am off from work tomorrow (today? Tuesday) so don't make noise.*

She was dreaming about reading Gogol in Russian when she heard the ringing of bells. Troika bells in the middle of summer? She opened her eyes. Three a.m. and the phone was ringing. That caller again? She picked up the receiver and held her breath.

A man's voice said, "Amalie? Amalie Price?" It sounded just like Ed Fielding.

"Ed?"

"Yeah, I'm sorry."

"Do you know what time it is?" It was pitch dark outside.

"That's why I'm calling," he said quickly. "It's three o'clock and I don't know where my daughter is. No joke." He had already called everyone he could think of. Then it occurred to him that Amalie's son might have an idea of where a sixteen-year-old girl might go. He'd come home from the Vermont trip and found his wife and daughter in the midst of a ferocious fight. When he tried to intervene Ellen had run out of the house. A girl that age wandering around in the middle of the night. His wife was sure she'd been kidnapped by a pimp at the Port Authority bus terminal. "I told her it was crazy to think like that but who knows."

"Of course it's crazy," Amalie said firmly, though it sounded perfectly plausible to her. The girl had probably gone to a friend's house to cool off. Easy to dispense wisdom about someone else's child, she thought. She would ask Charlie, though as far as she knew he'd never mentioned anyone called Ellen. The truth was that she could never remember the names of his friends, which enraged him.

Charlie's door was closed now and no light was showing. There was a backpack on the floor in the hallway. His friend must have arrived after Amalie fell asleep. She hesitated before going into his room. To awaken a sleeping child (or children?) has to be one of the crueler acts in life.

She returned to the phone. "I'll have to call you back. This will take a little time. What does Ellen look like? I don't remember the photo too well." She didn't mention Charlie's guest.

"Tall and skinny, fair wavy hair. She irons it every Saturday. To me she's very pretty but that's a father talking."

As she hung up she heard Charlie in the hall. He was on

his way back to his room, holding a glass of water.

"Honey, wait a second." Amalie put out her hand.

"Tired. Friend's thirsty." Charlie's eyes were barely open.

"Charlie, listen to me. Is your friend's name Ellen Fielding?"

Charlie opened his eyes wide. "What? Her name is Endive—pronounced the French way. G'night."

"I have to see her. Just for a moment. I won't turn on the light. I have my little penlight."

"That's *crazy*, Mom. My room is *private*. You don't just walk into a bedroom. I never did that to you." He went back into his room and shut the door.

Now what? Should she have insisted? Certainly not. But she put herself in Ed's place. She rang him, hoping his wife wouldn't answer.

"Yes?"

Amalie could hear his dread. Perhaps he was expecting a call from the police. She knew what that was like. "It's me. Does your daughter have a nickname?" Amalie explained about Charlie's guest and her reluctance to barge into the room.

"*Endive?* Jesus, what a dumb name. I never heard anyone call her that, not even her most spaced-out friends."

"Does she own a red backpack?"

"I have no idea. Her room is full of bags, hers, her friends'. They're always swapping. Carol—" he called to his wife, "did Ellen—it's Amalie Price. Amalie Price from work...I certainly have mentioned her name before, Carol. Please. Did Ellen have a red bag?" Pause. "My wife doesn't know. Maybe if I came over—no, that doesn't make sense."

Amalie had an idea. She could leave a note in the bathroom asking if the girl's name was Ellen and if so, to please call home. "I know I'm being a coward by not going into his room but I don't want to mess things up between Charlie and me." But then hearing how frantic Ed was, she said, "Okay, I'll do it, I'll go in there. This is more important."

"No, don't. It's such a remote possibility. I think your idea of a note is good. Maybe you'll be up before her, then you'll be able to see."

For the rest of the night Amalie tried to keep herself awake but at ten she awoke with a jolt. There was raga music playing and a heavy smell of wet plaster.

Charlie was in the kitchen wrapped in a towel, having just come out of one of his forty-five-minute showers that left paint peeling and tiles dislodged. There were pockmarks on the ceiling and puddles on the floor, left to dry naturally. The room was filled with a heavy mist since Charlie made sure to combine a shower with a steam bath. "Gets the poisons out," he always said, though where he had become so contaminated, Amalie had no idea. Now he stood in front of her, hair streaming, detoxified until tomorrow.

"How was Vermont?" he asked conversationally.

"Very beautiful, very quiet. Charlie—"

"See how friendly everybody is. Not like here. Could we get a jeep?"

"Sweetie, nothing's been decided. I have to think about it. Now about your friend—"

"She had to leave. I took down your note."

The phone rang and Charlie answered it, walking restlessly back and forth until the cord was wrapped around his body, a young Laacoon's. "…Okay, I'll distribute them from the Drive to Amsterdam. You take Columbus to Central Park West."

Now what was he hatching? Amalie had to get on the phone to call Ed and then needed to make a series of calls to finalize the plan for the tenant demonstration which was only three days away. "Charlie, I have to talk to you."

"Excuse me, mother, but I am on the phone."

"This is urgent."

"So's this—yeah—don't let the cops see you."

"Was it Ellen Fielding or not?" she demanded when he was off the phone.

"I'm taking the Fifth." he said solemnly. "I can't betray a friend. I'm not saying it was her—she. But just theoretically—"

"This isn't theoretical. If it is Ellen Fielding her parents are sick with worry. They're not evil people."

"No. That class of people are just incredibly conventional."

Amalie hated that self-righteous tone of his. But she was determined to keep her temper down. "I understand that it's a question of loyalty to your friend," she said. "But you have to understand—" Amalie swallowed "—where I'm coming from. If you disappeared from home in a huff and I didn't know where you were, wouldn't I be frantic? Like I was a couple of weeks ago? It was bad enough having to track you down at Criminal Court."

"That was different. It wasn't for personal reasons. God, look at the color of these flowers." Charlie touched a stalk of the freesia. "Purple is the most serious color."

"What am I supposed to tell Ed Fielding now?"

"Is he an all right dude?"

"Yes. More than all right. He's the chief editor where I work. Charlie, you are being recalcitrant on the basis of an abstract principle." Amalie was counting on the shock value of "recalcitrant."

"Principle is extremely important to me," he said stiffly. "Dad always talked about principle."

Amalie wasn't having any of that. "I'm asking you to put yourself in the position of a parent."

Suddenly his chin trembled. "Listen, listen—I have to

tell you something. You're not going to like this." His towel was coming loose, slipping below his neat umbilicus, their last link.

"Why don't you put on something first."

"You're always changing the subject." Charlie stomped out and returned soon after, dressed. "You remember my friend Endive?"

"How could I? I never met her."

"Oh yeah, I forgot. She—she's in trouble."

Drugs? Theft? Amalie took a wild stab. "She's pregnant."

He nodded, upset. "Her parents would freak out if they knew."

The phone again. Ed.

"Oh, I'm sorry I didn't get back to you—" Amalie started to apologize.

"It's okay. She's home, in one piece. Spent the night at a friend's, probably sleeping on the floor. That's what they do, these crazy kids." Not in this house, Amalie thought. Clean sheets and fluffy comforters. Ed's turn now to apologize. "It was a false alarm." Maybe yes, maybe no, Amalie thought, hanging up.

"Okay Charlie, this is serious business. Is your Endive's last name Fielding?"

"Why should I tell you. You might go and tell her parents."

"Charlie, are you—who's the father of this child? I mean of this child's child."

"I don't know," he said miserably. "I always thought the woman always knows who the father is. We only did it twice."

"Spare me the details. How far gone is she?"

"She skipped a period."

"Then there's no problem." Amalie was relieved. "She can get an abortion."

"Oh no," Charlie said, shocked. "That's out of the question. She wants the kid. And I agree. How can you kill a human being?"

"You're crazy, you know that?" Amalie shouted suddenly. "We're talking about a bunch of slimy cells."

"Would you say that if it was your grandchild?" he shouted back.

"Yes! A hundred times, yes. I'm too young to be a grandmother. You have to convince her. Someone has to. Her parents."

"They'd kill her if they knew. They're very bourgeois. Not like you and dad."

"Thanks a lot." Ed didn't exactly fit the bourgeois description as she understood it.

"She's going to need a place to stay when she starts getting fat," Charlie said.

Oh, that too. The Amalie Price home for wayward teenagers. "Honey, I think it's commendable to help out a friend," she said carefully. "But you're probably not to blame so why assume the responsibility?"

"She's counting on me. She's scared to tell her folks."

"Well, tough—" dropping all pretense at objectivity. "I can't harbor a girl here under those conditions." A girl who may be carrying my grandchild, a miniature Stewart perhaps.

"Dad would have said yes right away."

"Oh, he would even have helped deliver the child and made a movie of it at the same time." Even in death Stewart was still the hero, Amalie the heavy. Bad enough that he was the one who bought the treats and took Charlie to special places—a coal dumper in Bayonne, the Great Swamp. Not like boring old mom who could barely make it to the playground. Cut another notch in the tree, not the kind that celebrates growth, but rather the kind that digs into it in preparation for its fall.

"God, you're so hard hearted," Charlie said. "Don't you love little babies? They're so innocent."

"Innocent, my foot. They're fiendishly clever. Your N-Dive can't stay here and that's that."

"It's my house too, you know."

"To reiterate: I pay the rent." Amalie's ultimate weapon.

Charlie thought for a moment. "Okay, I guess I'll tell her that." He seemed relieved. "Thanks anyway."

"You're welcome, I'm sure," Amalie said, amazed at his turnaround. It just couldn't be true. She would try not to think about it. Compartmentalize, like men did. Little slots in the mind for different areas of life, with no overlap.

"Say, those flowers you bought are really beautiful, sweetie." She inhaled their exquisite smell. "Now, about the demonstration on Friday at City Hall…" She had to pin Charlie down because she might need his help. Many of the tenants in the building had promised to be there. Alex declined, however. He would hold the fort, crumbling though it was. Amalie was worried about having to take Friday off. She'd call in sick. But why should she worry about it. Her days at Berger MicroPubs were probably numbered. She was going to start checking the ads again.

"Maybe I'll be at the rally," Charlie said. "But maybe not. On the other hand, I probably will be."

His indecision was maddening. He couldn't ever commit to a specific time for anything in advance, though he seemed to be embracing fatherhood, all right. (Oh oh, that compartment had a leak in it.) Charlie always needed an out. One never knew when something more important might come along. The few times the whole family was obliged to be somewhere were an ordeal. He always kept his parents waiting and it was a relief to be able to say, when he was old enough, "Meet us there." The one time they had tickets to a play, he sauntered in during the second scene.

"Just say yes or no," Amalie said. "Will you leave with me promptly at ten a.m. or not?"

"What's the big deal about ten a.m.?"

"The big deal is that there may be changes in the line of march or we may need you for something else—to be a marshal, for example. Don't give me a hard time. Can I count on you, yes or no?"

"What are you so uptight about? Think positively."

"I *am* thinking positively. I'm thinking that I positively cannot stand your indecision."

"You're not exactly storming the Pentagon—yeah, yeah I know you went down to DC during Vietnam."

"A tenant march is small potatoes to you, isn't it."

"I didn't say it, you did."

"Oh God, wait till you're a parent."

Charlie gave her a crooked smile. "Maybe sooner than you think."

Chapter 10

On Friday morning, just before leaving for the rally at City Hall, Amalie remembered to call in sick at the office. "Oh hon," the receptionist said, "I know how it is sometimes. Getting out of bed in the morning is a lousy way to start the day. I'll tell her you have a flu."

In the lobby where the tenants were milling around, Mrs. Konarski was declining to leave her dog Genghis Khan behind.

"And suppose he leaves a load on the steps of City Hall?" 2D asked.

"There's so much crap at City Hall already, it won't make a difference," Rosetta Fineman said. "Ethan, what kind of sign is that, 'My Math Teacher Sucks'? Have a little respect."

The grass ruts kid had appeared and was attempting to address the tenants through a bullhorn even though they were few in number. He was exhorting them to chain themselves to the police barricades. Several tenants went back upstairs and refused to take part in the demonstration.

"We didn't ask for outside help," Amalie told the student angrily.

"But you want to do this professionally, don't you?"

She thrust some leaflets at him ("Tenants Si, Landlords, No," addresses of local legislators, which bills to support). He looked puzzled. "This is an outreach program to establish a proactive dialectic with the disenfranchised," Amalie explained. Ah—now he understood.

Several tenant groups had already assembled at City Hall Park when Amalie's contingent arrived. Despite the drizzle the atmosphere was festive. There were balloons and banners in many languages, representing neighborhoods all over the city. A handful of tourists wearing unbelievably clean pastels stared dully from behind the wooden barricades.

"What's the matter, you stupids." Mrs. Konarski shook her sign (SAVE RENT CONTROL). "They don't teach you to read in Myina-swota?" Her dog yapped encouragingly. He had ridden downtown inside her ruffled blouse and then leaped out at the subway station.

"I always wanted to see City Hall," Rosetta said rapturously. "Look at that golden roof. And how clean the steps are."

"Sure," someone said. "Black people sweep them every day."

Barricades had been set up all around City Hall, making it unapproachable, and the police were out in full force. Amalie herded her crew into a line. Too bad Charlie wasn't here. And too bad Stewart couldn't see her now. It wasn't much, organizing her neighbors for a march, but for her it was a daring change. Stewart would have been proud. Yes, Stewart, you would hardly recognize me now. I talk to lawyers and the press, I lobby Albany and call the mayor's office, I don't take no for answer. I would talk to God but as you know she's hard of hearing.

"Where are the songsheets?" people were asking. "You can't have a march without marching songs."

"I know some songs," Ethan Fineman said. "Do you know the one about—"

"—Get away from those holes, Ethan." Rosetta yanked his

arm. There were so many excavations around the park that it looked as though plans were underway to turn it into an island. Construction workers paused in their work and smiled at the marchers, a ragged group of about five hundred.

Amalie signaled to the student activist and he took up his bullhorn. "WHAT DO WE WANT?"

"HOUSING!"

"WHEN DO WE WANT IT?"

"NOW!"

Although she was shouting with the rest, Amalie disliked being on display like this. It was different during the anti-Vietnam war marches, strolling down Central Park West with Stewart and pushing Charlie in his stroller, sharing food with friends. This, with the drizzle and unfriendly tourists, didn't feel right. In the back of Amalie's mind was the thought that Hannelore would complain that she was falling behind in her work. Well, let her.

The crowd had grown along with the number of policemen in slickers. Amalie's group stalled momentarily as a network reporter bore down on her, followed by a cameraman. Amalie put on a welcoming smile. You had to be good to the media. In her calls to various newspapers and TV stations, she'd milked the human interest angle, identifying herself as a young widow (anything to get coverage), and giving capsule sob stories about some of the tenants.

"How about a statement?"

Amalie took a deep breath. "As you know," she began, "the Division of Housing and Community Renewal—DHCR— is in chaos just three years after its takeover of the rent regulatory system. Real estate firms are receiving preferential treatment, causing hardship for thousands of people. The agency is systematically violating the rent stabilization law and in fact is currently under investigation—"

"Hold it, hold it!" another crew member yelled. "We got some action starting."

Action? A group of people in wheelchairs and crutches had moved forward just as Amalie was about to launch into the provisions of the Emergency Tenant Protection Act of 1974 which she'd pretty much memorized.

Singing had started up:

> *Our mayor loves the landlords,*
> *He shall be removed.*
> *Just like the garbage in the harbor,*
> *He shall be removed.*

Some of Amalie's neighbors were arguing with a demonstrator ("Spread the Squatter Movement"). "We can't support that kind of thing," her people were shouting. "It's criminal trespass and it's wrong."

"Come on, gang," Amalie called. "This is politics. You make strange bedfellows…" Here was "Boycott Zucchini," *Succubus Magazine*, "Sisterhood Will Smash the State," Hispanic women joking with cops ("*Carne para los hombres!*"), the welfare families and women in furs (leaky luxury rentals). Futile though it might be, Amalie was feeling exhilarated.

"Why don't you folks go home?" a young cop asked her.

"Why not join us for a while?" she said. Oh Charlie, wouldn't you be proud of me.

"Look at all the little kids marching around in the rain," the cop said. "And all them old people. They should be home watching TV."

Suddenly a great cheer went up. Someone had appeared on the steps of City Hall. The sun came out at the same time. The police were narrowing the barricaded area, crowding the demonstrators onto the sidewalks. Traffic appeared to have halted in the neighboring streets. It was strangely quiet. Lights revolved gently around City Hall Park, the twirling orange or red lights from parked police cars, Con Edison trucks, telephone repair vans, highway maintenance vehicles—all equipped with beacons. The crowd faced the man on the steps, jockeying for position.

"Can everyone hear me?" The man's voice carried to every corner of the crowd. "They're cooperating up there," he said genially, pointing to the sky. Some people cheered. The man was very tall and even from where Amalie was standing it was evident that he was blooming with the kind of health depicted on packaged white bread. "My name is Howard F. Johnson and I'm the mayor's special assistant on housing."

Boos and hisses and calls for the mayor himself.

"It's a pleasure to talk to you today," Johnson said. Some of the demonstrators applauded. People will applaud for anything, Amalie thought. "I hope you'll excuse some of the construction. We're renovating the press wing and the work hasn't proceeded as rapidly as we hoped—"

"Get on with it…" The crowd was becoming restive. There were isolated catcalls.

Johnson rambled on about priorities. "…seems humorous of course that I should be telling you about the city's problems…"

"Stop the rent gauging," someone shouted. "Gouging, gouging," Amalie muttered.

People were straining against the barricades as the police warned them to move back. "Our children are dying…!" "Shame…!" "Open it up, open it up…!" The man on the steps could barely be heard now.

"Treating people like pigs!" screamed an elderly man, waving his cane.

"Revolution!" a child yelled. Ethan Fineman of course,

right next to Amalie.

The crowd surged forward. There was a crack and a roar. They had broken through the barriers, sweeping aside the police and moving toward the City Hall steps. The speaker backed up the steps toward the doorway.

Amalie found herself wedged solidly by bodies pressing against her on all sides. The marshals were yelling to the crowd to break it up. There was no way to move forward or backward. Amalie could see no further than the dandruff on the jacket in front of her. She couldn't even reach into her purse to pull out her smelling salts.

Ethan had begun to cry. "Stop pushing, stop pushing! I'm being squished."

Amalie grabbed his hand. "Hold on to me. We'll get out of here."

Police whistles were blowing. "Push hard," she said to Ethan. "Don't let go of my hand." Like a bull she butted through the crowd and toward the street.

"Watch out! Give the man some air..."

Me next, Amalie thought, sweating. Think of Ethan. Have to get through.

"Where's my mom? I want my mother," the boy was crying.

"Don't stop." She yanked him hard, tripping over people's feet, hearing curses. She could see the street, the edge of the curb. It was full of policemen, some with upraised billy clubs. The sun was blazing on their helmets.

"Look here, officer—" It was the bartender from 2A, gesticulating at a policeman who was holding Rosetta by the arm. "Aren't you exacerbating the situation?"

"Who axed you." The cop tightened his grip.

"Ma! Ma!" Ethan pushed his way to his mother.

"It's all right," Rosetta said nervously. "Amalie, get him out of here."

"I want to go home," Ethan sobbed. "I'm thirsty."

"You know the regulations," the policeman said. "You need a permit to parade on the roadway."

"I tell you I was pushed," Rosetta said. "I wasn't *parading*."

"Stepping off the sidewalk is an offense unless you have a permit. You're blocking traffic."

Amalie thought of Charlie. How frightened he must have been facing this same kind of obdurate force. "There is no traffic," Amalie said, wishing she'd been there for Charlie when he was picked up in front of Dow Chemical. "Be reasonable, officer."

There was no moving traffic, only parked vans and trucks, beacons revolving steadily. And now a throbbing noise filled the air. A low-flying helicopter. Was the mayor returning? The police were momentarily confused. The cop let go of Rosetta and stared at the sky. Ethan took advantage of his inattention to kick him in the shins.

"You little scum!" The officer yelled, grimacing with pain. "Grab that kid and take him in!" he shouted to the nearest policeman.

Rosetta screamed. "No! He's just a baby. Say you're sorry, Ethan, please."

The helicopter was circling. People were running aimlessly, trying to get away from it as though expecting to be sprayed with something lethal. "They're just counting us," Amalie said, but no one was paying attention. She managed to grab Ethan again and shoved him at Rosetta and the bartender. "Get away. Hurry." Then she sat down at the wounded officer's feet, right on the roadway.

"What the hell are you doing, lady? Where's that kid?" Amalie closed her eyes. When I open them, she thought, Rosetta and Ethan had better be gone. She could hear the helicopter and another sound. Drilling. All around City Hall they had begun to drill, digging deeper and deeper into the ground. No wonder there were so many construction workers. They were going to isolate the terrain and everyone on it. Amalie opened her eyes. Rosetta and Ethan had disappeared.

Two strong hands closed around her upper arms. "What's the charge, officer?" she asked pleasantly, twisting her head so she could see his face and badge number. If he broke her arm she hoped to faint immediately and then find herself in a private room in Mount Sinai Hospital, overlooking Central Park.

"Interfering with arrest and parading on the roadway."

As she was escorted into the police wagon she said, "You realize of course that in Gregory vs. Chicago—"

"Not interested."

She was handed into the crowded van filled mostly with people under thirty who greeted her with applause. One girl was crying. Amalie squeezed in next to her. "Don't worry, honey." She put her arm around her. "It's just a formality. My kid does this all the time. You'll call your parents. I'll call my son. In no time we'll be out of there. You think they take credit cards?" As the van lurched forward, she felt very sick indeed.

"Can I get you something else?"

"Charlie, stop tiptoeing around me as though I were an invalid. I'm just tired, that's all."

The phone hadn't stopped ringing but Charlie was taking the calls, mostly from other tenants, including Alex. He had made a few calls himself to friends, affecting a casual tone when he said that his mom had been in the clink. "Imagine what dad would have said." Charlie tucked a blanket around her ankles though it was eighty degrees.

"No big deal." Amalie was enjoying Charlie's attentions.

"Everybody gets arrested nowadays. Even fancy ladies who don't scoop up their poodle's poop." Easy to be blasé now that she was home in one piece. Charlie had been napping when she called him. Lucky he was home. He came down with whatever money was in the house, the $100 for groceries. She figured she could send him to the bank if there was going to be a whopping amount set for bail or a high fine. But the judge waved her away tiredly when her turn came—"Dear lady, go home"—and dismissed the charge. Amalie was somewhat offended. Perhaps he thought she had lost her way while shopping on Nassau Street. The processing had gone quickly for her, but they were being harder on the kids, fingerprinting them and detaining them for hours. She'd walked out with Charlie after three hours. He had seen a few of his friends there and seemed ashamed of having slept through the demonstration. There were no phone calls from Berger MicroPubs.

Mrs. Konarski stopped by with Genghis Khan. "Such a miscarriage of justice, they took you away, Mrs. Price. Always I wanted to see this place. We thought you were hippies when you moved here, may your husband rest in peace." Charlie was flipping the TV dial. "So much riffraff was there today. And the landlord persecutes people like me. I gave him at Christmas, I gave under the table, over the table…"

"Tell me, Mrs. Konarski," Amalie asked with sudden inspiration, "have you read Gogol? Can you teach me a little Russian?"

"Why you didn't ask me a few years ago? Now is no time left."

"Shh. I've got CNN. Look, mom, there's City Hall."

"I gave beautiful interview," Mrs. Konarski struggled to the edge of the couch. "They promised it for 6:30."

Over newsreel shots the anchorman described the crowd as mostly well behaved tenants whose spirits were undampened by the drizzle. (A groan from Charlie.) A few minor scuffles but no major incidents. "Which goes to show that you can fight City Hall. Chuck?" "Violence on the docks, startling testimony in the Iran-Contra hearings, and a breakthrough in space, after these messages."

At that moment the phone rang and Charlie picked it up. "Yeah," he said frowning, and handed the receiver to Amalie.

"Who...?" she mouthed but he shook his head.

It was Evan Diaz, calling to congratulate her. "Wow, you sure are telegenic," he said. "I happened to turn on the news and there you were."

"You want my autograph?" she said dryly.

"I was going to call you anyway. Are all your evenings tied up now that you're a star?"

"Pretty much." She really did not want to see Evan now. That last conversation with him had left a bad taste in her mouth. "I've got some people here, Evan, so I have to go."

"Sure," he said. "I'll catch you another time." I hope not, Amalie thought.

Mrs. Konarski was getting up to leave, disappointed and complaining about the outside agitators who were provoking the landlords, like that boy with the bullhorn.

He had called earlier to wish Amalie luck with the struggle. "If you need us, give us a call." Us is who? she wanted to ask but she was tired and the grammar was peculiar. Which reminded her again of Stewart's complaint that form was so important to her that it often held her back from life, from opportunities. But wasn't that so of Charlie who had held out for the perfect demonstration last week? Maybe that's why he hadn't gone to City Hall. He knew it would fall short. That didn't stop me, Stewart, she thought. You had me figured all wrong.

Chapter 11

On the metal cabinet containing duplicates of the company files sits a stuffed vulture, the bird being the official symbol of Hannelore's hometown in Germany. The tail contains a music box that plays "Lili Marlene." Marshall likes to listen to it sometimes when he and Hannelore are having sex in her apartment. She can never tell what kind of mood he'll be in.

This Friday evening, for instance, he hardly looks at her, undresses quickly, and before touching her says, "You should be seeing other men. This isn't healthy."

"I am not interested in the California style. I was not brought up like that."

Marshall laughs. "What do you know about California anyway. How about Frank McCullough? He's probably free."

"With him every word is filth. He is not a gentleman."

"Unlike me, right?" Marshall pours himself a drink, swallows it quickly and lies down. "No, don't take it off."

Hannelore glances at the clock. When he's finished, in about five minutes, she'll go down the list of staff names to see who is desirable and who is not, for the Vermont company.

"Is that good, baby—tell me, is it good?" Marshall always asks the same question.

"It's good, it's wonderful," Hannelore pants while thinking that it might be useful to try to retain Lisa the receptionist because of the Mafia connection.

"Show me you love it, baby. Move with me."

Hannelore moves and moans. "God, I love it…I am crazy about you, Marshall."

"Yeah, I know." He grunts and lets her go. "You have a great ass."

Marshall seldom compliments her. "You could have it more often," she says primly.

"Don't crowd me, baby," he warns. "It's just right this way. You might get bored otherwise."

"I have been thinking," Hannelore says a few minutes later. That's Marshall's signal to turn on the TV. Even though he respects and even fears Hannelore sometimes, her voice grates on him.

She mentions the comptroller's name. "But you can't let him go. He knows your accounts back and forth. He helped you with that real estate deal on Broome Street."

"Uh huh." Marshall turns up the sound. The news shows a demonstration in front of City Hall. An elderly woman holding a salivating Pekinese dog is being interviewed. Ah for the days of commitment. Where did he go wrong? He always turned out for these things when he was at City College. Sometimes his conscience quivers in the middle of the night, like an upset stomach. Though he gives generously to worthy causes, he is no longer a participant.

"Then we come to Najeed," Hannelore continues. You need her for the dirty work. We don't have to worry about her. She will never give up the job even if we move to Siberia."

"Look at all those people in wheelchairs—Jesus!" Marshall watches the screen intently.

"A bunch of crazies." Hannelore barely glances at the picture. "No respect for law and order."

There's a quick shot of a woman who looks like Amalie.

Come to think of it Marshall didn't see her in the office today. "Was what's her name at work today? Amalie?"

"She called in sick," Hannelore says, going into the kitchen. "Maybe she had a job interview."

"God forbid," Marshall says under his breath. He's remembering their awkward conversation early in the morning outside the hotel in Vermont. Amalie is probably one of those people who go through life unaware of the effect they have on others. He's watched her in the office, noticed her cordiality to everyone. She remembers whose kid is sick, whose husband has a heart condition. Although bereaved, she smiles at everyone. Doesn't show off her prodigious education. He wants very much to be in Vermont with her.

"I know how you feel about Ed," Hannelore calls from the other room. "You think he is indispensable but since we don't agree, I will not even mention him."

"Good." Amalie is like the sister he never had, the mother he wishes he had. A pal. A good-looking pal. He imagines throwing a ball around with her.

Hannelore returns with two glasses of Pinot Grigio. "You noticed of course that something funny is going on with those two."

"What two? Look at that—cops hitting a girl over the head."

"Amalie and Ed. They speak a lot together."

Marshall turns off the TV. "Stop making up dumb stories."

Hannelore smirks. "You told me to be observant, remember? Years ago. So I follow your instructions. There's something not—" she searches "—kosher."

"What do you mean, 'kosher'?" She does irk him sometimes. "Don't use words you don't understand."

"It's none of my business of course what the employees are

doing outside. *Die lustige Witwe*."

The Merry Widow. That's the extent of Hannelore's musical culture, Marshall thinks, putting off contemplating what she's just intimated. "I'm not interested in figments of your imagination. Go on with the list. What do you base that on, anyway?"

"They had lunch together once. Also she spends too much time in his office. And they sat together on the bus coming home from Vermont."

"People have to sit somewhere. Who's next on the list."

"Frank McCullough."

"Let's not count on him," Marshall says curtly.

Earlier in the day Hannelore had taken the telephone call from the Wisconsin Historical Society about the microfilms of their Civil War letters. Apparently the material shot by Frank was completely out of focus.

"Amalie is next," she says. "Theoretically what she does could be done by a couple of part-time people at a much cheaper rate and we would not have to pay benefits."

"We'll do everything to keep her. Go on."

Just as Hannelore suspected. Marshall has his eye on Amalie. Shame on her. The husband hardly cold and Ed Fielding a married man. Maybe something happened in Vermont. No, it couldn't have. She and Amalie had shared a room and it was only two nights. But maybe at some point during the day…? How long did it take to have sex, especially with Marshall, who was, from her experience, master of the quickie?

May the better man win, Marshall thinks, seeing Amalie in a new light. And it better be me. "You're my eyes and ears, sweetie," he tells Hannelore. "Remember that."

Sweetie? That's a new one. Hannelore hopes it doesn't preclude sex.

"We'll do the rest of the list on Monday. Offer anyone who

agrees to move a ten percent raise. Across the board." Amalie, don't waste yourself on that loser, Ed. I was the one who got him dried out and put him to work.

Marshall is fired up, thinking about those almond-shaped eyes, the straight line of those dense brows, the crazy possibility that she laid that body down on the line at the demonstration today. He's elated. He takes Hannelore's face between his hands, closes his eyes, and imagines he is with Amalie.

"I would do anything for you," Hannelore says, blinking back tears.

"Was that you?" Marshall asked Amalie on Monday morning.

"Where? When?" This was going to be a rough day for Amalie. There was a stack of work on her desk topped by a note written in letters as large as an exit sign: READ, SUMMARIZE, FILE, URGENT. H.

"City Hall. Friday. I saw it on NBC."

"Oh, I was watching CNN," she said evasively. He probably knew she had called in sick. "Look, I can explain." She hated having being forced to lie. Why should working at a job prevent you from exercising the few principles you had?

"We'll talk about it later," he said, going into his office.

Now she was in trouble. And here was Frank McCullough bearing down on her like a mad bull, that everlasting porkpie hat pushed to the back of his head. She pretended to be busy but he planted himself in front of her.

"Think you're so smart, don't you." He screwed up his eyes and leaned into her cubicle so that his face was inches from hers.

"I don't know what you're talking about, Frank." Amalie didn't need this today.

"Is it your business to go telling tales about me? Who told you to go snooping around the equipment room?"

This man was poison but she had never reported his mistakes, knowing they would be discovered eventually, like the outdated film and the cracked camera he used last week on the U.S. Naval Academy job, which resulted in ten rolls of microfilm with foggy images.

"The equipment room happens to double as a store room for supplies," Amalie said. "And I don't check for technical quality. That's supposed to be your job." She looked around to see who might be listening but there was no one.

"Look, babe, I've been in this business for years. I'm the expert here. You just stick to your fancy diddling on paper."

"Maybe you should try reading an instruction manual once in a while. And don't call me babe." Amalie raised her fist.

"Hey, hey, I like a feisty babe." He leaned in further, chin out, inviting her to strike him.

"Get away from me before I tell them that the FDR material came out backward."

"Who told you to open those boxes? That's my job."

"I wanted to check the captions. I wrote them, remember?"

Hannelore was coming towards them. Frank started to whistle and took off.

"Ah, you saw my note," Hannelore said to Amalie. "This should have been done a year ago."

"I wasn't working here a year ago," Amalie said. And may not be next week. That bastard Frank had shaken her up.

"I never stay home when I am sick," Hannelore said. "I hope you are recovered." That's hopeful, Amalie thought. It meant that Marshall hadn't let on to Hannelore that he knew where she was on Friday. "You are behind on the catalog changes. It holds everyone up."

"You really think everyone is waiting for me to change Zurich to Munich and 2nd rev. ed. to 3rd rev. ed.?" The wonderful world of minutiae.

Hannelore leaned down confidentially. "I have been meaning to tell you, Amalie. Lately you are distracted. You cannot let your personal life interfere with your work. Mr. Berger was furious with the mistakes you made in the *Book of the Dead* brochure."

"Which mistakes?" Amalie dared her to say but Hannelore merely shook her head. In the magnitude of mistakes any error Amalie might have made was as nothing. Frank McCullough was costing the company thousands of dollars, buying defective equipment and messing up the filming. Just because he played blues on the harmonica was no reason to be soft on him.

"I expected great things from you." Hannelore's mouth was wobbling. She turned her back and stamped back into her office.

The whole staff knew she was in a foul mood.

"It ain't the full moon, so what is it?"

"She isn't getting any, that's what it is."

"It freaks her out to have to move to Vermont. It's more than ten miles from Saks."

"I hear there are hyenas in Vermont. They come into the shopping malls. Sometimes they come right up to your car in the drive-ins. I rather stay here."

"You don't have drive-ins in Manalapan?"

"Shut up, you fruit. I'm not kidding about the hyenas. My brother-in-law was at a drive-in and he sees this thing through the windshield? He thought it was part of the movie. I swear to God."

"Don't swear. The Pope's in town."

All day Amalie waited for Marshall to call her into his office for a dressing down. She would not, absolutely would not complain to him about Frank's behavior.

Reprimanding Amalie, however, was the furthest thing from Marshall's mind. He really wanted to crown her with roses. Guts is what she had. Whereas he—? Marshall was disgusted with himself. He no longer even signed petitions. Amalie reminded him of what he used to be. How could he approach a woman like that? For the first time he was at a loss about how to talk to an attractive woman. He could summon her to his office to do the managerial thing and chew her out over the phony sick day. But that would be hypocritical. Maybe they could talk about the medieval medicine treatise—but that would be poaching on Ed's territory. Hannelore must be wrong about her suspicions about those two. Ed was too passive. He'd never make a move.

Why not call Amalie in to discuss the relocation? No, that wouldn't be fair. He didn't want to put pressure on her. I'm her boss, damn it. But that was no consolation.

Here is the perfect solution, Hannelore was thinking, brooding over her mail. When Ed to the National Library Convention goes (she was thinking in German) we send Amalie with. Remove two sources of irritation. You needed at least two people at the booth. She herself was barred from this convention by Ed and Marshall, in the same way that the editorial office was off limits. She and Ed had carved up the conventions between them, just like the great nations of Europe. Keeping the balance of power.

"I saw you on TV," Ed said to Amalie as he encountered her at the xerox machine. No mistaking that admiring tone. By now she was embarrassed. She hadn't been in danger, had not been hurt. It was, in fact thrilling. I can do this, she thought. It feels good. I understand the logistics, the forces, the politics. I could hold my own now in any argument with Stewart.

"It was just a cameo appearance," she said to Ed. "Let's

not make too much out of it." If I were sincere, she thought, I'd work among the poor. Then she remembered the man on the subway with the loud boombox and how angry she'd been at the disturbance. And for a moment she was ashamed. Poor guy, no job probably. Wait a minute—let's not get maudlin and romantic about the poor like Stewart used to do.

"I understand we're going to the NLC," Ed said. "The National Library Convention in Yuma City."

"Who's we?"

"You and me. One person minds the booth while the other one hustles."

Amalie smiled. Just the two of them. Anticipation wafted through her like a Caribbean breeze. The last time she'd been to a professional conference was as a newly-minted M.A., to sniff out job possibilities. Networking they called it. She'd do the same thing again, only this time she had some experience under her belt.

Chapter 12

"Let me shake the hand of a celebrity." Ralph Dobrin wiped his fingers on his apron. "I saw you on the news."

Amalie was on her way home from work when Ralph rapped on his store window and motioned her in. The place was empty except for the helper who was sweeping up. "Hey Hoolio," Ralph called to his assistant. "Mrs. Price here was on the news on Friday. Maybe you want her autograph. Assuming—" he whispered when the boy declined "—he knows how to read. He's a great kid. We understand each other. All it takes is a little effort and goodwill for people to get along. I'll give you an example. I'm not keeping you, am I?"

"My son's waiting for me." Not for the first time Amalie wondered if Ralph was given to making anonymous phone calls.

"I won't keep you long. Hold on a second." He quickly changed a couple of prices in the display case with a black marker. "Cost of living increase," he explained. "So, like I was saying. Last winter my car got stuck on the thruway in a four-foot-high snowdrift. A car comes along and stops. Would you believe a purple Lincoln? A real pimpmobile. But smart. Chains on the tires. These two black guys get out and ask me why I'm standing there in the middle of the highway. Can't move, I say, but with a little help…You should have seen that Lincoln."

"Ralph, I really have to go." That stack of marrow bones was beginning to look sinister.

"I'll make it short. I see these two big guys and I say, 'Fellows, we can do it. With my brains and your brawn we'll show everyone how we can work together.' In a nutshell they put their shoulders to the car and shove. Those guys are made of steel. My car starts to edge out of the drift. 'Great, you got it' (I encourage them to give them a little spirit). And that was it."

"Too bad it got stolen." Amalie edged toward the shop door.

"I got myself a better car. Japanese. Keep it in the garage. Honey, do me a favor and take these chops to the old man."

In front of Amalie's building Elisha the superintendent greeted her with a bare-fanged smile. "Your son he's come and gone. He said he forgot his key."

"Why didn't you let him in?" Amalie was furious. "Don't you have emergency keys to all the apartments? It's the law."

Elisha waved his screw driver, an ominous addition to his already unsavory person. "No more laws for this house. House belongs to someone else, someone else got the keys. Soon everybody get a dispossess and I get me a new job with a uniform." And closed-circuit TV so you can spy on everyone, Amalie thought.

Today is the day, Alex thinks. What matters is to make a decision, right or wrong. Yesterday a piece of debris had struck him on the head. Perhaps it was a piece of the Russian Kosmos vehicle that had disintegrated up in space. Like the Revolution it had gone off course. Remnants were supposed to have fallen to earth and this one had fallen through the clouds in the vicinity of the Central Park Zoo and glanced off his head. It hadn't hurt. At first he thought it was a piece off the cornice of the lion house. But he knew it was no ordinary piece of debris because it had struck at the source of his perception. The first proof was an immediate revelation that gorillas were beautiful. Then he felt a benevolence emanating from every creature in the zoo.

And this morning when he stepped outside for his morning constitutional he had the distinct impression that many of the people who passed him on the street were in love. Alex knew without asking them. Furthermore he realized that most people were in love, requited or not. Imagine the ramifications for history. Along with greed and the need for natural resources and access to the sea, governments could be motivated by love. He was not naive enough to think that love was uppermost in everyone's mind—obviously not, given the state of the world. The only person who would truly understand the concept was a thinker of the stature of Amalie's father, Herb Marcus, the eminent sociologist, his old buddy.

Was Amalie also in love? Who was the lucky man? Alas, he himself was out of the running. Still…Oh God who does not exist, send Amalie up for a short visit.

The efficacy of prayer was immediately demonstrated as Alex's doorbell rang.

"I knew it was you." He took the bag from Amalie and brought it to the kitchen. "Stay a bit, my dear Scheherazade. Remember when I was ill and you rang the bell every day to see how I was?"

Amalie was embarrassed. "It's nothing special." He seemed to have poured on a gallon of sandalwood aftershave. Though it was supposed to drive a woman mad, it was merely clogging her sinuses.

Alex took her hand. "Yesterday I was struck on the head and saw the light. Love is all around us." He paused meaningfully.

Oh oh, it's either Jesus or me, she thought.

"Is it shameful, a man my age?" He was still holding her hand.

"Of course not, Alex." He would make a perfect godfather, though Amalie hoped the necessity would not present itself.

"Oh how your life has changed," he reminded her, gently guiding her to the couch. "Now you're in the public eye, playing a heroic part...Surely you're ready to branch out?"

The sandalwood was getting to her. Alex was one of her favorite people. Not for the first time she wondered what sex would be like with a man his age. She could pretend it was Stewart. No, that was morbid. Try imagining it's Ed Fielding.

"You see, then I can die happy." Alex spoke as though she'd been following his train of thought.

"It's not a matter of dying, Alex."

"I have every intention of dying," he said stubbornly.

"Stop this crazy talk. Honestly, Alex, I just want to shake you sometimes. Look at this piano, full of dust. When was the last time you sat down and played?"

Alex looked away. "I've been getting my affairs in order." He took a handkerchief out of his pocket and gave an ineffective swipe at the keyboard. "Do me a favor," he said. "Tell your father, my old friend, to come and visit. That will shake some sense in my head. A man with his intelligence."

Amalie doubted that her father's presence could have such a beneficial effect on anyone. "I'll pass on the message," she promised. Right now she had no idea where he was and didn't really care.

Hannelore had insisted that Amalie and Ed take separate flights to the National Library conference. No sense taking a chance on losing two employees simultaneously. Since Ed's plane had been delayed Amalie set up the booth on the convention floor, spotted some likely sales prospects, and chatted with the dashing bibliographer from the Library of Congress who reminded her that they had a date to look at his incunabula. It might be worthwhile, she decided, if he could steer her to some library executives with big budgets. Berger MicroPubs had just completed filming a collection of programs and prompt books from the Elizabethan era as well as some American labor ephemera. Perfect for that Ohio university library.

Hold it. What was happening to her? She was turning into a company person just when she was contemplating leaving. Was she going to lose her soul? What would Stewart have said. Well, Stewart, I'm having fun doing this, believe it or not. And you also were a company man though your employer was the English department at Columbia U. Good thing Charlie wasn't around now to jeer at her identification with "the oppressors."

Like the pyramids of Egypt the convention center cum hotel was set in the middle of a desert. "Ozymandias," Amalie thought when she first set eyes on the buildings from the air. Bereft of ornamentation, two slabs rose sixty storeys high, reflecting only each other. Shelley's lines came into Amalie's head. "…*Round the decay / Of that colossal wreck, boundless and bare / The lone and level sands stretch far away.*" Visible from afar, as church steeples used to be, the towers provided only illusory relief from the flatness of the landscape.

The sterility of the exterior was deceptive. Inside was a hotbed of hedonism, if not downright debauchery which seemed to be promoted as the best way to get the job done. Hospitality suites were everywhere, every organization was issuing invitations to parties, gifts were being handed out—shopping bags, calendars, bumper stickers, books, T-shirts, mugs. An island of diplomatic immunity where there were no censors, bosses, or spouses to monitor behavior. This freedom from obligation must have been what Stewart enjoyed when he went to his conferences, though she hoped it was tempered by a little guilt,.

The revolving rooftop lounge, with a seventy-five-mile view, was the perfect place to start something. Amalie could suggest it to Ed. Then they'd see. But what about his wife? Yes, what about her? Maybe they were experiencing some problems. Amalie was glad she'd never met her. She was still an abstraction, to be respected or ignored (or both). The worst thing would be to meet her and to find that Ms. Fielding was a charming, vibrant person. ("You'd like her," Stewart often said when speaking of a colleague, which immediately sent Amalie's antennae up.) But there was another problem: suppose Charlie's putatively pregnant Endive was indeed Ed's daughter. Sleeping with Ed could be viewed as a novel form of incest. Interesting concept. She'd float it past him. Easy to make up scenarios while he was still airborne.

Amalie was at the booth, writing up an order placed by a librarian for the complete novels of Benjamin Disraeli on microfiche when Ed appeared.

"I saw the mini-series," said the librarian who was wearing a gardenia in her hair, "but you're the first person I've met who's actually read any Disraeli."

"Just a fluke," Amalie said.

"You're too modest," Ed said when the woman had gone. "Take credit whenever you can and cc the boss. Don't you want to climb the corporate ladder?"

"I'm looking for a shortcut," she said, then realized he might misinterpret what she meant. But the clod Ed smiled at her and praised her for having done so much already, singlehandedly.

He complained about the small print on participants' badges. "I find myself staring more than I usually do at women's bosoms. How else can I decipher their names?"

"You could ask."

"This way is more fun."

Please feel free to stare at mine, Amalie felt like saying.

The booth was quiet now and Ed suggested she take some time to visit some of the other booths or attend a panel discussion. They hadn't figured out who would do what and she didn't want to cramp his style so she agreed to leave him alone for a while. Maybe later she'd take him up to the revolving lounge.

There were a number of choices for this time slot. "Heuristic Reasoning in the Sentient Anfractuousities of Ross MacDonald," "The Role of Kitchen Novels in the Literature of the South Jersey Shore," "The Virgin in Doonesbury Culture," as well as "Stasis and Iconography in Clint Eastwood's Cinema." And here was a session on "The Failure of Alterity in the 'Ballades' of Christine de Pisan." Well, Amalie didn't know about the alterity part, but the Ballades were beautiful. She closed her eyes and remembered: "*Seulette suy, en ma chambre enserrée / Seulette suy, sanz ami demourée.*" I'm all alone, locked in my room, alone without a friend…No thanks, she'd skip that panel. Out of nostalgia, maybe she'd pop into a talk on "The Gaze of the Other in Translinear Empowerment: Pornographic Comics as Transgendered Praxis."

The meeting room was packed, standing room only; the place seemed to have been sprayed with Bombay Gin room freshener. The lecturer had projected some slides depicting nude figures in various slippery poses and was reading the French captions and then their English translations. There was something familiar about those texts. Of course. Amalie had done the translations. The lecturer was not attributing them to anyone. On the one hand Amalie was indignant. Shouldn't she be given credit for the work? On the other, did she really want to be identified with it? Her credibility here as a representative of a staid academic micro-publisher would be nil. "*Je ne veux plus entendre*," she murmured, shoving aside a mouth-licking Francophile from Catholic University in Washington.

Next, she walked into "Spatial Entropy in Aristotle's Poetics" in the middle of the first panelist's presentation. It was very warm in the room and the atmosphere was one of somnolence. The presenter seemed to be reciting a long poem and sweating profusely. "Cognitive and tutored reflection," he said and paused. "Landscapes of the grasped given…" Amalie glanced at her program. The speaker taught poetics at Tampa State and had several books to his credit. "Organized praise transmutes into a Socratic debriefing…" Pause again. "We must want to look," he said in a choked voice and looked beseechingly at the audience of eight. Maybe he was hoping that someone would offer him a drink of water. "Clarity," he begged and waited for a second or two. "Helping us to optimize psychic dissonance." Again he paused. Then he crumpled his papers and sat down.

A hand shot up. The questioner, a young woman in a flowing flowered skirt could barely contain her awe. "How did you determine where the pauses would occur in this work? And how did you choose what specific words would follow the pauses? It's—" she couldn't contain herself "—a brilliantly structured innovative piece of work about the narrative gaze."

The presenter mopped his brow. He probably wished he was back in Tampa where the air conditioning never broke down. "Truthfully," he said in a choked voice, "I'm always so nervous when making a presentation that I have to stop after every few words to take a deep breath. It's just stage fright." He smiled wanly.

"Oh you're just being modest," the flowered girl said as Amalie left the room.

When she returned to the booth, she suggested that Ed take off and make some rounds but he seemed content to remain in the small space with her.

"Does your wife mind your being away from home?" she asked, fussing with some brochures.

Ed took a while to answer. "Let's just say that lately there's been an absence of domestic felicity."

"I'm so sorry." Amalie meant it. There was nothing to be gained from his unhappiness. And she didn't want him on the rebound. But why kid myself, she thought. He hasn't made a move in my direction. But from booth to bed was not such a long way. She tried it mentally: booth, boot, bolt, belt, bet, bed. It was the only word game she'd ever played because she always won, beating Stewart the English teacher handily.

"Your admirer from the Library of Congress came by to invite you to a workshop on—pardon the expression—'Oral Knowledge: A Confabulation of Tongues.'" He showed it to her in the program index. Just above it was "Oral History as Reflexive Sociology," due to start in a half hour.

That sounded like something Amalie's father might have devised. Yes, there he was, listed as a consultant. Amalie wondered if he was here with his latest inamorata.

Not many people were stopping by the booth, many probably had started their serious cash bar activities. Ed checked his watch. "How about dinner later. I hear there's a revolving restaurant."

"Sounds great," Amalie said, "but I don't need to be entertained."

"Call that entertainment? Last year a bunch of periodicals people went skinny dipping in the hotel fountain."

Was he trying to titillate her? She certainly wouldn't mind skinny dipping with him but not with 500 library administrators. They agreed to meet later for dinner in the revolving lounge. And since Ed insisted on staying at the booth and wrapping it up, she took off for the Oral History session, looking forward to surprising her father.

The conference room was dark when Amalie slipped into a seat. The whirring of a defective 16mm projector was going to be a problem if one was to understand the narration of the sound track for *Ojibwa Sands: The Timeless Return*. The only light in the room came from the tiny gleams made by the penlights of people taking notes though only the main title had appeared on the screen. Wouldn't her father be surprised if he knew she was actually looking at some of his work.

An American Indian chant, poorly recorded. If I close my eyes and then open them again, Amalie thought, there will be a desert, a highway, mountains, and cactus in close-up. Oh so predictable—except that there is no cactus. The music breaks off abruptly. Cut to the interior of a ramshackle house, the kitchen dominated by a large television set.

Off-camera narrator: "We're talking with Estelle May Ojibway. You can see her preparing tea in her Fargo, North Dakota kitchen." Zoom in to mangy dog asleep on a rag rug. Sounds of clattering dishes, a voice coming probably from the television news describing a twister that has just uprooted eight mobile homes. "Bill, can you bring the camera in a little closer so we can see Mrs. Ojibway making tea?" (What's the big deal? Amalie thinks. This isn't the Japanese tea ceremony.)

Camera jiggles, then focuses on gnarled fingers holding a commercial teabag. Man's voice: "Git that thing outa my face."

Zoom in to very old cheerful dark-skinned woman. The upper part of her head is cut off on the screen (scalped—the cameraman's revenge?).

"When did you come to North Dakota, Mrs. Ojibway?" (Title on bottom of screen says "Pseudonym.")

The old woman laughs heartily. "I told you already."

"Tell us again, for the benefit of the audience."

"I come to North Dakota in the year…" (she is facing what she thinks is the camera but she is in profile) "…in the year of the blizzard."

"When was that exactly?"

"Where did you put your ears? I just told you."

The camera swings over to the perplexed interviewer, a nervous young man fingering his lavaliere microphone as though it were a rosary. Maybe he's worried about the tornado which, judging from the sounds coming from the TV, is approaching the woman's kitchen.

"What did your father do?"

"When?" Now she is seen full-face. She's drinking beer out of a bottle and a cat seems to have found the tea cup.

"What kind of work did he do, Mrs. Ojibway?"

"You call me Estelle, my American name."

"OK, Estelle, tell us what kind of work he did."

"Smith."

"Smith? But I thought—one second, we're having a little trouble with the equipment. Bill, can you just untangle—"

"He had a forge."

"Ah—" with evident relief "—he was a blacksmith. You know that poem, Mrs. Ojibway—Estelle? 'Under the spreading chestnut tree, the village smithy stands…'?"

"Plague took the chestnut trees that year."

"Tell us about it."

"Cheyenne come and raid the farms."

"Cheyenne! What happened?"

As she starts to speak, Herb Marcus's voice comes on, overlapping that of the woman. "The twentieth century is very much in evidence here…" The familiar pompous tone, the slight accent.

"…Cheyenne raid burned up all the houses—you like tepee better?"

"…with television and the latest pickup truck." Cut, of course, to the pickup. Either the camera or the earth is trembling. "The elements have not been kind to this area," Professor Marcus continues.

"Those fellas come on horses and lassoed my little brother. One of them picked me up and carried me across the river."

Herb Marcus again: "In 1960 there were seventy-five farms here. Now there are only four."

"This fella, he took me to his village and tied me to a tree—" With sudden inspiration, the camera pans to a tree right outside the door. "—Then he paints my face. And then they give me something sweet to drink. Taste like Pepsi Cola. I had a good time."

Herb Marcus takes over with a list of statistics about health, employment, family structure. His German accent seems more pronounced than ever. Maybe that's what happens as people age, Amalie thinks.

Now the first narrator: "Thank you very much, Mrs. Ojibway—Estelle." He recites the credits, details about sponsorship, locations, names of laboratories—all of which are already listed in the rolling title. Fadeout with the sound of glass shattering (Mrs. Ojibway's beer bottle?).

The lights went on. Amalie's father stood in the doorway and was immediately surrounded by well-wishers.

"His work is so cutting edge," said the woman next to Amalie. "I feel privileged to be exposed to it. Oh, he's looking this way. Maybe he remembers me from the last conference."

But Herb had spotted his daughter and broke away from his admirers.

"Hi, Dad. I figured I'd see you here." Amalie was torn between wishing she had left before the lights came on and wanting to hug her father.

Herb Marcus was a tall bony man with a sallow complexion.

One side of his face was a little caved in as though, in passing him by, life had dealt him a terrific blow. He stretched out his arms. "My God, here's my little girl." Always performing for the audience, Amalie thought. The amphitheater of students, the graduate assistants, the corporate moguls who forked over thousands of dollars to find out that their secretaries liked to have plants on their desks. Even as he embraced his daughter, his eyes were searching the room.

"Did you come with a friend?" Amalie asked, disengaging herself.

He pointed to a young woman in her twenties who was busy rolling up some wires.

"You remember Fiona, don't you?"

"Ah yes, Fiona Ransom. 'Re-Visioning Mega/Meta T-Group Dynamics.'"

"Such a good memory!"

Amalie also remembered that when Stewart died her father took off right away after the funeral, to which he was late. "Forget all this," he had told her. "Don't get morbid." His idea of condolences. He went away with some Fiona-like girl, away from unpleasantnesses like death and reality. Because Amalie's grief didn't fit any of his statistical studies.

"How did you like Mrs. Ojibway? She's part of the cohort for my comparative study of Native American families. It's my first oral history."

I can tell, Amalie almost said, but he wasn't interested in her reaction since she wasn't obviously complimenting him. But others were coming up and shaking his hand. "Great movie…" "A landmark…" "It'll be part of the canon."

Amalie's father turned to her again. "What are you doing here?" he asked. "Are you training to be a librarian or what? The three of us should have dinner. Fiona, I don't think you've met my daughter."

The diplomatic Fiona said, "He talks about you and his grandchild so often." Playing it safe, didn't say grandson because she probably wasn't sure of the gender.

"Are you his secretary?" Amalie asked. "There was a time when my dad felt all women should become secretaries or grade-school teachers."

"I've done a little teaching," Fiona murmured. "Just an introductory sociology class.

"I fooled him," Amalie said. "Instead of secretarial work I did porno translations. Dad, remember how you'd read me the secretarial ads at the dinner table?"

Herbert chucked his daughter under the chin. "Times were different then, *Liebchen*. Isn't she lovely?" he asked the remaining bystanders, though Amalie didn't know if he was referring to her or to Fiona, who trailed them out of the room.

"Alex Dobrin! He's your neighbor? I can't believe it," Herbert said.

It was fortunate that Amalie had agreed to have dinner later with Ed in the revolving restaurant. The most she could endure now was a cup of coffee in the overpriced hotel cafe.

"I would give my egg teeth to see him," Herbert continued. Fiona was keeping a straight face. "But tell me, Amalie, are you seeing anyone?"

She decided to ignore the question. "Why don't you call once in a while. We never know where you are. You could have come to Charlie's graduation."

"Now you are not being fair, Amalie."

"Herbert," Fiona said, "I think I'd better leave you two together."

"Stay, Fiona," he said. His hands were shaking. "I don't like to worry you, Amalie. Fiona has looked after me, thank God. If not for her…"

"He had a triple bypass," Fiona said proudly.

Amalie gritted her teeth. Beware the guilt trip. The maximum allowable capacity has been exceeded. She tried to control her voice. "Don't you think it's incumbent upon you to notify me, your next of kin, when there's an emergency?"

"He didn't want to upset you." Fiona was speaking for both of them. Herbert was swallowing hard. Was that a tear in his eye?

"Damn it, Daddy." Amalie punched his shoulder awkwardly. "For someone who studies human nature, you have some terrible blind spots."

"Didn't I send Charlie a present? For which, by the way, I never received an acknowledgment. In my day you would send thank you notes, but far be it from me to interfere in the upbringing of your son."

"Yes, very far, as far away as possible," Amalie flared up. "You took off for Malaysia the day he graduated though you could have put off the trip. He was so hurt." That was a lie. Charlie understood far better than she. "The old man can't stand real emotions, that's all," he said. "They scare him. That's why you could never argue in your house or yell or criticize. What we do is much healthier." "I wonder," Amalie had said. "I really wonder," thinking of the many slammed doors and Charlie's tears.

Fiona had had enough and excused herself. Herbert looked around wildly. He seemed fearful of being left alone with his daughter.

"You're not going to pull another heart attack on me, are you, Dad? Though I imagine that Fiona is an expert at CPR." Surely that was in her repertoire of physical skills.

Herbert leaned forward and lowered his voice. "How are your finances? Do you need any money?"

"Sweet of you to ask. Am I one of your statistics, one of the newly widowed with no visible means of support, a likely subject for a study by one of your mediocre assistants?"

"*Liebchen*," Herbert groaned, "go easy. I'm an old man with not many pleasures and very little to look forward to."

"Well, here's something." This was going to be fun. "You may be on the verge of becoming a great-grandfather."

Herbert swore in German, reverting to his native language. "This is impossible. How old is the boy."

Another black mark against him. He didn't even know Charlie's age. "Old enough to fuck."

Her father winced. "There is no need for that kind of language."

"Okay. Old enough for sexual congress. Come on, Dad, I know you'd rather talk about the latest films but you might try participating in family life as it is lived instead of reducing it to charts and tables."

Herbert sat back, frowning. "I don't recognize you at all, Amalie. You used to be such a lady. You've changed."

And a good thing it is too. No longer jelly, no longer to be pushed into a daughter mold, a secretary mold, a wife mold.

"You've become so—aggressive."

"You're changing the subject, as usual."

"No, no, I remember what you said. I might be a great-grandfather some day. I would like that."

"Not some day. Maybe in seven months if all goes badly." Amalie told him about Charlie and Endive who didn't know who the father was. In any case, Charlie refused to entertain the idea of an abortion. "If it's Charlie's we are up the creek. I am not about to play nanny."

Herbert patted her hand. "It would not be the end of the world."

"For Christ's sake, Daddy!"

"What has happened to freedom of speech?" Herbert looked under his chair.

"For your information, my building is about to be demolished and I may have to move to Vermont if I want a roof over my head. So there." Amalie was regressing, she could hear it, see it in the way she was twisting her napkin.

"The house is going down? What will Alex do?" Herbert wondered. "He's not the type for a retirement community, that rascal."

"Maybe he'll also move to Vermont," she said sarcastically.

"Yes, why not? Maybe I will also. Maybe we can all be in one big house."

"Yeah, Fiona can do the baking."

Her father blew his nose. "It would be wonderful to have a little baby in the family. You grew up too fast, too fast. Before I knew it you were married. And now, I am old and tired." He slumped down in his seat.

Amalie was alarmed by his heavy breathing and the pallor of his face. She touched his arm.

"It's this business of running from one conference to another," he said. "The film, the slides, the questions. Let's face it, I made my splash a long time ago. All this is just to keep busy. You know I used to be skeptical of extended families, but there is a society on Ossabaw Island—"

"Vermont is not Ossabaw Island."

"Ah you catch on, you were always clever. You should have been a social scientist."

"One per family is enough. Are you really suggesting that we all set up housekeeping in Vermont? You, Alex Dobrin, Fiona, Charlie, the Endive, baby and me?"

"There are many definitions of family in the world. This arrangement does not strike me as unworkable." Herbert had a gleam in his eye.

"You're cuckoo, Daddy." For the first time, Amalie laughed.

"Think about it. There are precedents. I'll give you a reading list. Consider it seriously before you go killing off your own flesh and blood." He looked at his watch. "You haven't really told me how you're doing."

"You didn't really ask. I'll tell you next time we meet." Amalie slipped out of his hug and waved at Fiona who was waiting for Herbert at the entrance. She had to dress for her heavy date with Ed.

Chapter 13

About half a mile from the Biblio Haunt is an old wooden bridge connecting two Vermont towns. The bridge is constructed of planks that are lashed together, but many of them have loosened and decayed over the years and there are great gaps between them. When the river swells, which happens with almost every heavy rainfall, the water level rises above the roadway. At one time there was enough play in the structure to allow the bridge to float and move slightly with the motion of the current. There is a sign on both banks advising motorists and walkers to cross only at their own risk.

Driving slowly on the road leading to the bridge, Marshall was thinking that the locals would be won over gradually. He knew how resistant they were to change, especially if initiated by outsiders. This was the cradle of American civilization and Marshall was determined to have a piece of it. If you could bring jobs into the area, that would be a real contribution and you'd be respected.

"Is it okay to cross?" he asked a couple of fishermen in slickers when he reached the bridge. Water was sloshing over the roadway and it was raining hard.

"It's always wet. Meant to be that way. We cross even when it's a foot deep. It don't hurt the car as long as you got good wires." They leaned their poles against a barrier and crossed their arms. Daring him?

You jokers, he thought. It reminded him of all the those challenges met and unmet in the alleyways of Jersey City. This was going to be his territory soon. He'd gotten it fair and square, all the papers signed. Berger MicroPubs of Bristow, Vermont.

The two guys nodded encouragingly. Another car crossed quickly from the other side, the driver waving to the fishermen when he reached the bank. A couple of boys on bikes zigzagged across, barefoot on their pedals, tires parting the waters, like the Israelites with the Red Sea.

Marshall pressed down on the accelerator, letting those fishermen hear the sweet sound of a Jaguar. No one knew he was here today. Not even Hannelore who would have wanted to come along. He needed to see the land again, alone, unhampered. He wanted to stay in the hotel where he and Amalie had been under the same roof. She seemed to fit in so well with this landscape even though she was, like him, a city kid. Now he was sorry that he'd agreed to send her to the library convention with Ed. They'd surely end up in bed together. What was it about her? Amalie had that quality you can't name that fills out an empty space, adds color and movement, air.

Marshall began to drive across the bridge, imagining Amalie crossing with him some day, walking, holding hands. The car shook with the movement of the bridge. The water seemed to be rising, as though a sluice gate had been opened. As he reached the midpoint the car shuddered and stalled. On the bank behind him he could see through his rearview mirror the two fishermen shaking their heads and motioning him to move on. He couldn't tell if those mothers were laughing or not.

Come on, baby. He pumped the gas pedal and tried the ignition several times, but all he got was a nasty whine, like a cranky baby's. Jesus, what a time to stall. What was he supposed to do, swim across? He wasn't about to abandon this brand-new beige Jaguar on the bridge. A motorcyclist was revving up on the opposite bank. He was going to try and make it across. But no, he must have changed his mind for he wheeled around and took off. Marshall got out of the car and stepped into six inches of water. Son of a bitch. Too late to take off his shoes. He waded to the front of the car and opened the hood. This would be a distress signal on the highway but this was no highway.

The water continued to rise. A group of people had gathered on the bank he'd just left. They were making swimming motions at him. Why the fuck didn't any of them come and help? He could swear they were laughing. He'd look like a damn fool if he climbed to the roof of the car and sat there in the rain. He couldn't see the roadway any more and the water was rising fast. It was almost up to the door handle.

A terrific wind had come up now. This is the country, Marshall thought. This is what you want, the bucolic life. You could drown here and none of those clowns would try to save you. For the first time he was afraid. He was a poor swimmer, afraid of deep water. He never went in over his head. He always needed to touch bottom.

If he started walking across he could probably make it before the water rose above his head. This was a damn stupid way to build a bridge, with flimsy guard rails on either side. A short person would be swept right underneath and into the river.

The water was up to the side mirror, up to Marshall's chest. He felt his jacket dragging him down, clamping him to these rotted planks. He arms were paralyzed with cold and his teeth were chattering. Take off something, lighten the weight. Like an idiot he removed his watch and placed it on the roof of the car. He managed to remove his jacket and tossed it on top of the car.

"I can't swim!" he shouted and waved his arms. The group on the bank turned around and took off, away from him. In a second not a soul was left. They don't want to see it, not their responsibility. My will is in order, Marshall thought, hanging on to the door handle. Trust fund for the kid, no debts, no regrets. Except that I've never really been in love. Then Amalie's face came into his head. His eyelashes were wet, the wind was blowing rain into his eyes. Amalie, smiling, encouraging, *do it, do it…*

He cast himself off, pushing against the car with his hands and feet. Then he raised his knees. For a second he was floating. Like the bridge…then he began to swim clumsily toward the shore he'd just left.

With a tremendous effort he kicked off his shoes (loafers, fortunately). Now he could hardly see the shore because of the growing darkness. He was afraid of letting his legs down to test for bottom. He might panic. Now he was maintaining a steady crawl. *Amalie*, he thought, *bring me through it.* He said her name each time he gasped for air. *Do it for me, bring me through. I will love you, Amalie. I need to make it across.* He found himself crying, "God, let her help me."

A strange prayer, he realized later. Just when he thought his strength had given out altogether he touched the muddy bank and dragged himself up. For a moment he lay on the ground with his eyes closed and rain pouring down on him. When he finally sat up he could no longer see the car.

While Marshall was struggling to keep himself from drowning, Amalie was sitting in the revolving restaurant with Ed, drinking scotch and getting dizzier and dizzier. They should build in some stops in the restaurant's mechanism, she thought.

Suppose you had to go to the ladies room. There would be no way to orient yourself by looking out the window, not that there was much distinction between one highway strip and another. Ed seemed glum. "Talk to me," she said, resigned to hearing about his domestic problems.

"My daughter," he said. "But you don't want to hear about that."

"Is she pregnant?" Amalie asked, thinking of her putative grandchild.

Ed didn't seem surprised at the question. "It's drugs," he said. "We thought she had stopped. But as an ex-alcoholic I know how hard it is to break a habit."

How come he was being so open with her? If Amalie hadn't heard it from Marshall she might have reacted with surprise. Now, all she said was, "I understand," thinking how lucky she was that her child didn't have a drug problem, as far as she knew.

Ellen had been grounded for a month so Ed didn't have to go calling all over town to find her. "I never apologized for bothering you that time. We were desperate. But now I feel sorry for my wife who has to deal with her. Sometimes she's just too hard on the girl."

Amalie noticed that there were some white hairs in his eyebrows. Very appropriate for a man who saw life in shades of grey. She wanted to distract him from his troubles. They could distract each other.

She took another swallow. "Were those mountains there before?"

Ed laughed softly. Here was a man who surely knew his topography, like Stewart. There was a big king-emperor-sized bed in her room. *The wife, think of the wife.* Amalie was a wife and did it stop Stewart? She'd never know.

"I may be a grandmother soon," Amalie said. "That's why

I asked if your daughter was pregnant."

"You? That would make you the first thirty-year-old grandmother in the microform business."

Oh the darling man. "I'd hope these kids would avail themselves of modern science and get an abortion," she said, her stomach lurching.

"Oh no," Ed said. "If it was my kid, I'd be against it."

So that's how it was with him. One would have thought that a person with his views on semiotics and the killing of baby seals would have views compatible with hers. No, Amalie would not go to bed with such a person. She had her principles. Not that he had evinced the slightest interest. Amalie leaned forward, squeezing her elbows against her body and folding her hands, giving him a good view of a cleavage that was invisible under ordinary circumstances.

"Your food is going to get cold," he said, digging into his monkfish.

She looked at her mussels and gagged. The room was turning at an accelerated rate.

Before she knew it, Ed had his arm around her waist and was leading her into the elevator. How clever of him to stop in front of the door to her room. How did he get her key? Wasn't there something she was planning to do tonight? Like seduce him? Amalie closed her eyes. "I spoiled it," she said.

He led her into the room. "Here's your bed. I'm taking off your shoes."

"What a screw-up," she murmured. There was an elevator sliding up her insides.

"There'll be other opportunities," he said, kissing her forehead and covering her with the bedspread. "It happens to everybody."

Opportunities for what? she wondered when she awoke with a horrendous headache. But maybe he had ravished her in her sleep like in that German movie, *The Marquise of O.* But no, judging from the cheery face that greeted her at the booth, nothing had happened. It probably never even occurred to him. She realized that Ed was one of those people with whom you had to be very explicit. You'd have to say: Let's do it. He reminded her of one of those mastodons in ice. They look fresh, alive, no parts missing—but impossible to get at. Maybe she'd try again.

Hannelore's first thought on awakening was that Marshall was trying to kill her. It had always been a possibility, ever since he found out about his Hungarian cousins, killed at Bergen-Belsen. She couldn't imagine a more satisfying way to die than to expire in Marshall's arms. The feeling seemed to come from the dream she'd had in which someone presses her face down on the glass top of the xerox machine. A light flashes in her eyes, there's a whirring sound, and a picture emerges from the feeder of a negative face with glowing white holes where the eyes are supposed to be.

There was a lot of rage in Marshall but he was sure to mellow after they moved to Vermont, Hannelore thought. In the country he would lose his bitterness, forget history, and become imbued with the spirit of nature. Like Wagner's Siegfried, he might even understand the language of the birds. But no—he had enough trouble with German.

He was not going to be pleased this morning when he found out that subversive forces had been at work over the weekend. A complete set of Bulwer-Lytton microfiche was missing from the office. Hannelore had a pretty good idea of who the thief was and planned to unmask the person during the 11:00 staff meeting. Only Ed and Amalie were exempt from suspicion since they had been away. From the way that

Najeed was tiptoeing around, ashen-faced, finger on her lips, one would have thought she was the culprit. The place was strangely subdued today. Marshall's door was closed. He'd apparently had some trouble with his car during his last trip to Vermont.

The office boy was nursing a black eye and the comptroller was brooding about balance sheets and euthanasia. He was eager to move to Bristow where he would find kindred souls, small towners like himself who went to church and owned guns. Only Irina was cheerful as she chattered in Polish over the phone. In a year she would retire and open up a knitwear boutique in Lambertville.

When Amalie arrived, Hannelore threw her arms around her. At the same time, Marshall flung open his door.

"What's happened?" Amalie asked. "Did we finally sell a complete set of Bulwer-Lytton?"

"Not quite." Marshall rocked on his heels, smiling benignly. The sight of the two women hugging seemed to warm the cockles of his heart.

The volumes had been stolen, Hannelore explained. There was a big hole in the B-U-L section of the stockroom upstairs. She planned to expose the criminal publicly.

Marshall continued to smile. There was a faraway look in his eyes. "And the waters made way…" he murmured.

Had he gotten religion all of a sudden? Amalie wondered.

"Someone is sneaking around 'borrowing' our materials," Hannelore said.

Oh oh, that Gissing book was still on Amalie's night table, an 1896 edition.

"Don't worry about the Gissing book," Hannelore said. "We are not ready to film it. I know you return everything."

Marshall was looking at Amalie peculiarly. "Of course I'm returning it," she said. "I didn't think I had to sign it out."

"Hey, it's one of the perks. Forget about it," Marshall said, motioning her into his office. "Come tell me about the conference. Was the blonde from Norwich College there? They just got a bequest. Did Ed take good care of you?"

What kind of question was that? "He was very good to work with," Amalie said stiffly. "And no, Norwich College wasn't there but the guy from Simon's Rock is ordering the complete Peabody-Trask essays. When did you discover that the fiche were missing?"

"Hannelore says she knows who it is. I don't know if I like the idea of doing this in public at the meeting."

"Of course not," Amalie said. "You're the president. Do what you think is right. Talk to the person in private. What do you need a hit man for?" Then she caught herself. She'd gone too far. Who was she to give him advice? "Look, I didn't mean to get carried away."

"You are absolutely right," Marshall said. "You're demonstrating real executive potential. With some coaching you could really move up in this company, especially when we expand. In feminist books you know that they advise every woman to find a mentor in her professional life."

"I'll keep that in mind," she said. "How come you're reading feminist books?"

"I like to know what goes on in minds like yours."

Oh, how far off he was. Unless a feminist book had some elegance of language to recommend it, she was apt to shun it. At least that had been so in the past when style seemed to be more important to her than substance.

"About the Bulwer-Lytton," Marshall continued, "Hannelore's probably mistaken. The materials could have been misplaced." You couldn't read microfiche or microfilm unless you had the right equipment anyway. "Hannelore has a tendency to exaggerate when she's under stress."

Hannelore under stress? And what about me, Amalie thought, having to decide about Vermont or looking for another job? And possibly on the verge of becoming a grandmother? Maybe Ed's daughter was telling him at this very moment that she was pregnant. It would not be a coincidence, Charlie would say. It's karma. It was meant to be. Please let it not be Ed's daughter, she thought.

At the staff meeting, Hannelore sat apart, tight-lipped. Marshall had taken Amalie's advice and told Hannelore that there was to be no public accusation. He'd handle it in his own way. He reported briefly on the prospects for the company, its relocation plans, new markets, cost projections. As though, Hannelore was thinking, any of these people give a damn. Weed them out, get rid of the bad apples. Enough about the myth of democracy. She glared at the comptroller. Him with his phony British accent. Thief.

Ed reported on the library conference. Amalie, he said, deserved most of the credit. She'd buttonholed important people, scouted out new projects. "Tell them, Amalie," he said like a proud father.

How about the peace pamphlets housed at The Hague which had never been microfilmed, she said. Also, a cache of disintegrating documents about the Choctaw Nation in a warehouse in Oklahoma, just waiting to be preserved on film. And the State Department was dying to have their correspondence with the British Public Records Office put on microfiche and distributed to academic institutions worldwide....

Just listen to yourself, Amalie was thinking as she talked. I would hire a person like me. A new résumé was taking shape in her head. Her other thought was that she could ask for a whopping raise now and might even get it. If they wanted her in Vermont they would have to make it worth her while. After all, there might be Daddy and Charlie and baby and Mommy and God knows who else in one big house.

On the way out of the meeting, Hannelore complained again about the missing set of microfiche. "Is not missing," Irina said, surprised. She had come in late. "You told them upstairs to ship quickly to Harvard History Department. No invoice, nothing. I told you it messes up my records."

"Your records are always a mess," Hannelore snapped and made for the ladies room.

"Sometimes she is a little crazy," Irina said to Marshall. "Ask the stock boys upstairs."

"I believe you," he said, not at all disturbed. He seemed to be enjoying the fuss. He took Amalie aside. "Nice work. You and I should—"

"—Not a good idea," she interrupted. "Let's not blur the lines. Management 101."

"You could teach the course," Marshall said admiringly and went back to his office.

Whew! Amalie thought. My mouth said "no no" but my heart said "*si si.*"

Chapter 14

"Have you been discussing my personal life with grandpa?" Charlie accosted his mother as she came in.

"Whose suitcase is that?" Amalie had almost tripped on it, her view obscured by the groceries she was carrying.

"Grandpa's."

"Grandpa's? What's he doing here? Where is he anyhow?" He hadn't let her know he was coming. All it would have taken was a simple phone call. But no, Herbert Marcus felt free to ignore the most basic social courtesies where his daughter was concerned.

"He just went up to Columbia but he'll be back." Charlie said. "What did you tell him?"

"Did he say he was going to stay overnight, or what?" Amalie couldn't imagine what had brought on this urge on her father's part to spend time with his family.

"Mom! I asked you a question. Did you discuss my personal life with him?"

"Of course not, sweetie. But wouldn't you rather talk seriously with him than have him ask you about baseball or what you want to do when you grow up?" But of course Charlie *is* grown up, Amalie thought.

"You told him, didn't you. About my friend Endive. I know you did. Because he gave me this long lecture on the joys of parenting, then he talked about abortion being a sin. I can't believe you violated my confidence." Charlie's voice was getting teary.

"He's your grandfather, he's not a stranger." But he might as well be, for all the interest he usually took in her and Charlie.

"Suppose he tells other people and then her parents find out."

"Oh stop being paranoid." Amalie was sick of the men in her family. Her father, her son, and even Stewart the holy ghost. Not to speak of Marshall Berger. They were going to drive her nuts, all these guys. "Well, I'm starving, I've had a hard day at work." Not strictly true. She had surreptitiously typed up her résumé. It looked pretty impressive even to her.

The answering machine was flashing. "Who called?"

"How the fuck would I know? I don't listen to your messages. I happen to have some consideration for a person's privacy."

The message was from the Mayoral Task Force on Housing. Amalie had come to their attention as a possible candidate for the assistant administrator's position. They were accepting resumes. Her name had been passed along to them by the official at the Department of Housing Preservation and Development who'd helped dig out her landlord's records for her second appeal—they had spoken a couple of times—and by Evan Diaz. Aha, guilty conscience, Amalie thought. Trying to make amends for his betrayal, giving the developer information he should have kept to himself. No use, Evan. You, the urban historian, are history in my book.

"Wow!" Charlie said, apparently forgetting about his impending fatherhood. "We could stay in the city, then. They probably get box seats to all the Yankee games."

"Don't be dumb." Amalie was amazed that the housing official even remembered her after all these months. He must have assumed that she was more qualified than she was, or else he just liked the sound of her voice.

"You could bluff it," Charlie said loyally. "With all the tenant stuff you've been doing?"

"'Tenant stuff' does not constitute a résumé." But how great that Charlie was finally beginning to appreciate her. "On the other hand, I just typed mine up and it looks pretty good. There's a lot about organizational transition and managing innovation in a new team environment."

"Sounds a little like grandpa."

"It's in the blood," Amalie said. "Now help me unload these groceries, will you."

A note on the refrigerator door caught her eye. "Charlie, what is this note—'Herring'? Have you stopped being a vegetarian?"

"It's '*Hearing.*' My court hearing is on Thursday, in two days. I hope you didn't forget. I told you the date fifty times."

"Thursday? A work day?" She had no recollection of Charlie telling her the exact date. But then she didn't always listen to him carefully.

"I told you. It's at ten o'clock. You have to be there. In case…" his voice cracked "…in case I'm sentenced to jail."

The doorbell rang.

Arms outstretched, a beaming Herb Marcus. "My little girl!"

"What are you doing here?" Amalie said while Charlie uttered a shocked, "Mom!" Trying to recover her manners, Amalie said, "You could have let me know. Your timing is not exactly great."

"Yes, I know, we have a hearing on Thursday." Herb said smoothly. "Charlie called me in New Haven and I took the train down."

Charlie actually called his grandfather? "Is this true,

Charlie?"

"Sure, why not? The family has to stick together in times like these."

Herb was smiling broadly.

"Oh, terrific," Amalie said, yanking open the refrigerator door. "Here's another entry for *Ripley's Believe It or Not*."

The bell rang again.

"Ah, that will be Alex. I called him from the station."

Yet another mouth to feed. Amalie needed to be alone with Charlie to talk about the court date. Suppose he was sentenced to a jail term? Yes, Stewart, your fondest hopes realized. No, I'm sorry. I'm just pissed that you're not here and that a woman's scarf was found in your car.

Herbert opened the door. "Sparafucile!" he exclaimed.

"Celeste Aida!" Alex cried. "Our old passwords." The two men fell into each other's arms.

"This man saved my life once," Herbert said.

"I have no memory of that," Alex said. "You're making it up like you make up all those theories I read about." He blew his nose conspicuously.

"My daughter wouldn't be here today if you hadn't dragged me out of that foxhole at Messina."

"It was Cassino, Herbie."

Leaving them to pummel each other affectionately, Amalie steered Charlie to the kitchen table and pushed him into a chair. "Now, about this hearing. Nothing's going to happen. Don't worry. This is America. We'll get the best lawyer."

"Don't be ridiculous, Mom. We already have the best lawyer. Fowler. You met him."

"How do you know he's the best?" A barefoot lawyer with a dog named Amicus.

"He once spent two years in a mental institution and when he came out he wrote an exposé about the rights of mental patients and the laws got changed."

"Some recommendation. Who hired him anyway? Say, could you keep it down in there, please," Amalie called into the living room. She'd never heard her father laugh so hard.

"The Movement hired the lawyer," Charlie said. "They know what they're doing."

"Will you know what to say? Did the lawyer coach you?"

"Relax. Did you know that Gandhi did his best writing in prison?"

"So did Hitler. You know, I could strangle you sometimes, Charlie." The mention of Gandhi brought to mind Marshall Berger's sinister white suits. Did he think they endowed him with special powers, like a shaman's outfit?

"See," Charlie continued, "what they don't know is if they give me a suspended sentence, I'm going down to Guatemala to join the student compañeros."

"You'll do no such thing!" Amalie said loudly.

"Shhh. Mom, please. They'll think there's something wrong."

"Of course there's something wrong!"

"Do you need help?" Herbert ducked his head into the kitchen.

"Everything is just fine," Amalie said through clenched teeth. "God's in his heaven and all's right with the world."

"That's my little girl," Herbert said gaily and retreated to the living room.

"Where were we?" Amalie said. "Oh yes, the student compañeros. First of all, except for that one gym class you're no longer a student."

"I'll register for a class at the Learning Annex. How to talk to women or something like that. Maybe the judge will make me do community service. I'll tell him about the teenage hotline."

Amalie could see that Charlie was worried too. Of course. How could he not be? She leaned across the table and planted a kiss on his forehead.

"Don't worry, Mom. They always dismiss these cases. You'll meet Endive on Thursday." Charlie was actually blushing. "She's afraid to see a doctor. She bought a pregnancy test kit but she couldn't figure out the instructions so she threw it away."

"And she's still not sure who—?"

"It would be nice to know," he said wistfully. "I want Grandpa to meet her too. Just in case. He'll be there in court. I asked him to come. I don't think you really appreciate him enough, Mom."

"You didn't grow up with him, OK?" She slapped some plates down on the table. Paper plates it should have been. Who am I trying to impress?

"Well, you turned out all right, didn't you?" Charlie said, squeezing her hand. "You are the best."

Happy news, she thought, for however long it lasts.

"Are we going to eat soon?" Herbert called from the living room. Then he said, loudly enough for Amalie to hear, "Listen, Alex. Maybe some day we'll be roommates again. Remember Fort Dix? You snored so loud…"

"I was composing in my sleep but you were tone deaf."

When Amalie entered the courtroom on Thursday morning, the lawyer Fowler glared at her, probably still irritated because of the doubts she had expressed about his ability to bring the case to a successful conclusion. She was terrified of what might happen to Charlie. She didn't believe in the system any more. What was going to happen to her boy now that he had chosen the path of most resistance?

Several rows in the courtroom were filled with junior high

school children, here to watch democracy in action but mostly to stare at the guards' holsters. It was stifling in the room and Amalie was fighting the urge to nod off. She hadn't gotten much rest since her father arrived, trying to keep track of his comings and goings and worrying about today.

"I have a trumpet card," Herbert said when they discussed Charlie's hearing. "Even you will sit up and take notice."

A door opened and a group of young people filed in. There was Charlie, flashing a victory sign at Amalie and pointing to the girl behind him. But all Amalie could see was a cascade of blond hair descending to her coccyx. Mother of my grandchild? Future daughter in-common-law? The two kids had met when they climbed a fence together outside a nuclear installation. Grounds for a lasting relationship.

Please don't let them go to jail, Amalie prayed. Just give them a chance. I'll take in the Endive and the child. I'll find work, two jobs if necessary. She remembered the phone call from the Task Force on Housing. She would polish up her résumé and send it to them. Downplay her literary background and Berger MicroPubs experience. JOB OBJECTIVE: *Position of Civic Responsibility.* QUALIFICATIONS: *Familiarity with NY Housing Code and agencies; HPD, DHCR, NPP, HUD*—wasn't that a movie with Paul Newman?—*HDA, recent Appellate Court Decisions, Section 8, "order to correct," maximum base rent, Senior Citizen Rent Increase Exemption.* "Tenant stuff," as Charlie put it. Just right for the Task Force on Housing. On-the-ground experience with tenant issues, conflict resolution...If Charlie was sentenced to a jail term, God forbid, she would need all the pull she could muster. Though "Housing" didn't exactly mean the housing of prisoners.

"All rise."

The judge's gavel brought her to attention. Charlie had said he would join the student compañeros in Guatemala.

He might be safer in jail. The matter was out of her hands. You can't control everything, Stewart had said. But he would have tried anyway. The lawyers and assistant D.A.'s had been summoned to the bench. After a couple of minutes they burst out laughing. What could be funnier than deciding a person's life? She noticed that her father and Alex Dobrin had come into the courtroom. Fowler handed the guard a note which was given to the judge.

Amalie's father was going to testify as a friend of the court and expert witness if there were no objections. The judge was looking straight at her. What was her dad trying to do? At worst he might jeopardize Charlie's case. At best he would just embarrass everyone.

Herb Marcus was holding a pack of notes. In the old days he could speak extemporaneously for hours. His memory must be failing. He was obviously nervous. Oh Daddy, she thought, strangely moved. You don't always have to be perfect.

After being sworn in, Herbert Marcus began to speak. He said he would first provide some background, and began to describe his childhood in Munich, "a city not known for its civil liberties. When I was seventeen the Nazis deported all the Jews. I was strong and so I was sent to work in a munitions factory."

Amalie was stunned. She felt her heart racing and she seemed to be having trouble breathing. Why, why had he never told her any of this? All she knew was that he was orphaned by the time he came to America. Whenever she tried to get him to talk about his youth, he always changed the subject and she had stopped asking after a while. The only past he was willing to talk about seemed to begin with his enlistment in the US Army during World War II.

"I engaged in sabotage at the munitions factory," he was saying. "I made sure every other bolt was defective. I did it because I believed in justice. These children here believe in justice. They are not harming society. On the contrary." He was in total control of the courtroom. Amalie could see why he had built a reputation as a mesmerizing teacher. Not a paper was rustling in the room.

I don't understand, she was thinking, wiping her forehead and trying to piece her father's life together. US Army corporal, super patriot at home who brooked no criticism of anything American. Justifying the most deleterious government decisions through the use of sociological research and arguing ferociously with Stewart who stopped talking to him after a while.

Fowler rose to question him, as an expert on family mores. "Given the fact that law-breaking could be construed as rebelling against the larger social family..."

What in God's name did this have to do with Charlie blocking pedestrian traffic outside of Dow Chemical? Amalie's father was now making some of his typical pompous pronouncements, even mentioning genetic codes. Yeah, like Stewart's activism was imprinted in our son.

"Suffering can be ennobling," Herbert was saying, his eyes popping with emotion. As though he was a better person for having suffered. What nonsense. He lost his parents. He was a slave laborer as a teenager. There was no purpose in suffering, Amalie thought, picturing her father as a skinny orphan boy with Charlie's eyes. Daddy, she thought, breaking out into a sweat, Save Charlie if you can even though no one saved you.

"And finally..." Herb delivered an emotional paean to the First Amendment, reciting it as though it were the "Song of Songs," and bringing tears to Amalie's eyes. When he finally stepped down from the stand, she stood up, wanting to go to him. But her legs wobbled and the back of the bench in front of her seemed too near her face. She motioned to the nearest guard. "I think I'm going to faint," she whispered.

Amalie was lying on a bench outside the courtroom. Alex Dobrin was holding her hand, looking pretty pale himself. Several guards were looking down at her. Someone was fanning her. Alex said, "Your dad had to go. He had an appointment. A date," he added, making a face. "He'll call later."

Still woozy she sat up. "The hearing. Where's Charlie?"

"Here I am." Charlie knelt on the ground beside the bench. "It's okay. Everything's okay. We got dismissed with a warning and a five-hundred-dollar fine. Your dad paid it. Why didn't you ever tell me about him? He's such a cool guy."

She put her head between her knees. Bless Mr. Fowler the lawyer. Bless the Movement for hiring him. Bless the system when it works. She would write a note of thanks to Mr. Fowler as soon as she got home. And she had to talk to her father.

"Ma, this is Endive." Charlie motioned to the longhaired girl dressed as though she was about to parachute out of a small plane.

"So you're—Charlie's friend." She just couldn't say that vegetable name. "What's your real name?"

"Ellen Fielding? Charlie said you work in the same place as my dad? Ed Fielding?"

"I think," Amalie said, "I'd like to be left alone. Please everyone go away." She began to cry with relief. Her son was safe, for now.

"Come, child." Alex helped her up. "I'll take you home."

Stewart, Stewart, why did you have to go and leave me?

Chapter 15

Alex tipped his hat to the wrecking machine parked in the lot next to his apartment building. Its head was raised like an giant insect's, waiting to pounce. In the moonlight it glinted seductively. He could imagine its great teeth chattering ecstatically like castanets on a giant calliope. But the sound that accompanied him through the streets tonight was a muffled beating of bongo drums. There was trash under the benches on the Broadway mall, the surest sign of spring. The tents were gone from the grassy sections, the saffron-robed hare krishnas had decamped to 34th Street to bang their bongs in front of Pennsylvania Station.

Alex wandered over to Columbus Avenue, cutting through the low-income project, shabby even in blueprint, past the decrepit public school which Charlie Price had attended before the tortuous rezoning that redirected the kids in Alex's building to the newer whiter school on West End Avenue. Columbus had undergone renewal of earthquake proportions. Although there were still pockets of bodegas and three-storied corniced brownstones inhabited by the last stickball players, huge supermarkets and boutiques were opening every day. The shadow of an unfinished thirty-story condominium lay over a parking lot that used to be a community garden. Prognathous balconies overhung the rubble-filled street.

Alex's son was pressing him about Fernmeadow Estates.
The destruction of his apartment building seemed imminent.
Many of the people had relocated, including Amalie Price. All
the rallies and petitions had come to naught. Now Ms. Price
was working in the very office that controlled these decisions,
the Mayor's Task Force on Housing. Oh she was a hard one,
all right. Gave up the fight as soon as she got the job half a
year ago. The corruption of power. Her housing worries were
over. As soon as she got that new job she was offered one of the
apartments the city had set aside for select employees.

Alex could give in to his son, move to the retirement home,
embrace canasta, bingo, and those harbingers of pestilence, the
social workers. Or maybe move into one of the new efficiency
apartments for the elderly the city was building so fast they
forgot to put in closets. All the numbers and letters would be
giant-sized like in a cartoon and there would be guardrails on
every wall, in case he wanted to practice ballet—"No, Pop,
they're for holding on to." They'd make him share his living
quarters with some old geezer who would fill the refrigerator
with prune juice and leave his dentures in a glass in the middle
of the kitchen table. Herb Marcus had been the ideal bunkmate.
He didn't snore and they played chess every night. But that was
over forty years ago.

Alex waved a salutation to the moon. In my veins, he
thought, the moon organisms. Free, I hope from the litter we
have strewn about the Sea of Tranquility. The cars faced him
as though he were the speaker at an emergency meeting, side
mirrors gleaming like the corner of an eye, catching flashes
from other eyes around them. He wouldn't know Ralph's car if
he saw it. One car in particular caught his attention, pearl grey
with whitewall tires, like a distinguished gentleman in spats,
which Alex had worn only once to a dance contest. Something
scurried past his feet and he shut his eyes. Well, you have

wildlife in the country too.

"Sssst!" It was a little kid, about ten, crouching near the fender of a Buick in the lot.

"What are you doing," Alex called.

The kid straightened up. "I didn't do nothing."

"You better go on home. It's very late."

"I can go where I want." A clanking noise made Alex look around.

"Shit," he heard a voice say. Two other kids bobbed up over the hood of a Mercedes. They were bigger. One of them was holding what had been a car's antenna.

"You got any money," the first kid asked him.

Alex began to perspire. "I don't have any money but I have music in my heart."

If he got out of this he would make an important life decision.

A blond Hermes from Federal Express delivered a videotape to Amalie's office just as she was about to step into a staff meeting. Her father's name was on the envelope, which had a Vermont return address. She'd look at it afterwards.

It was getting on to five o'clock and one major issue still hadn't been resolved at the meeting. Stewart used to complain about bureaucracy at departmental meetings at Columbia but those were just a pale simulacrum of what went on at city government agencies, as Amalie had found out. She had doggedly continued to pursue the case against her former landlord, tracking it through labyrinthine offices, putting what amounted to a "tail" on it in the person of the housing official who had been so helpful to her originally.

"I'm going to get you," she often muttered to herself and sometimes people looked at her strangely. The case was interfering with her sleep and with her sex life. Talk about being distracted. Whoever she was with—Skip Fowler, Charlie's former lawyer, or the charming philanthropist who was interested in preservation—would be startled to see her sit bolt upright in bed, fists clenched and cursing the real estate industry.

Even though Amalie no longer lived there, her old building deserved to be saved. Alex was still there though he seemed to be harboring a grudge against her, as though she had deserted her neighbors. There was no point in telling him that she was still fighting to save the house.

The pesky item on the agenda for the staff meeting concerned a mouse that had been spotted under a locked file drawer in Amalie's boss's office, the drawer that probably contained all his inept attempts to write coherent reports.

Presiding over the meeting while puffing on a pipe, her boss said, "I suggest forming a small committee to study this—pest problem." The office manager, a desiccated male who had memorized every New York City statute on the books objected. According to some obscure bylaw, other divisions on the floor had to be consulted first.

Amalie shuddered. By the time the group came up with a recommendation, there would be whole colonies of mice in every office. "What about poison," she said.

Several people looked at her with horror. There were some animal rights fanatics among them.

Her boss cleared his throat. Amalie knew it was to his advantage not to antagonize her. The man had been a communications major which meant that he'd watched every sitcom since the 1970s in a luxurious amphitheatre on the campus of Boca College, but still hadn't learned to spell. He knew that someone would always clean up his work, which Amalie did, thereby fulfilling her father's hope that she become the assistant to a male executive who in this case was the son-in-law of a City Council member. In exchange he left her alone most of the time. But it galled her that he took credit for reports she wrote.

Now he said, "I resonate with both approaches, but there is the push-pull factor."

What in God's name was the idiot talking about, Amalie wondered and looked at her watch. People were being thrown out of their homes every hour, inspectors were being bribed, fires were breaking out because of faulty wiring, and these people were dithering about a rodent.

"Folks," Amalie said when there was a pause, "let me tell you how my father dealt with the problem." Funny that she should remember for the first time something that happened when she was a child.

Her father would set a trap before going to bed, she began. In the morning he would approach it "obliquely, you might say, just close enough to see that the mouse had been caught. You see, he first put on a pair of dark glasses." Then he would take one of her mother's hand-embroidered handkerchiefs and drop it over the trap. (Amalie could see that her colleagues were fascinated.) Next, he shoveled up the trap, which was covered by the handkerchief, into a paper bag and threw it out the window which faced the alley. Her office mates looked scandalized. This was one of the very problems they had to deal with in the slums. *She lives in a slum*, Amalie could imagine them thinking, but so what. "Oh yes, then he'd announce that there had been a death in the family. Are we finished?"

"Maybe," said the timid receptionist, "I could bring in a have-a-heart trap. It wouldn't hurt the little fellow and then we could release it somewhere."

"First of all, which budget would it come out of?" demanded the office manager. "And second, where would the mouse be released?"

"How about the mayor's office?" Amalie said and scraped back her chair. "I think we've got our methodology squared away now." There must be a special bureaucratic gene, she thought, remembering the old tenant meetings and people like Ms. Fanchelle and her panic about touching the mail.

In her office, she slipped the video into the machine.

Against a musical background of country fiddling the video opens with a shot of a good-looking young man atop a tractor, waving and churning up the ground. Charlie, during his last visit to his grandfather in Vermont. A year and a half after relocating to Vermont Berger MicroPubs has expanded into audiotapes, videos, slides and software, and Herbert Marcus, the eminent sociologist, has become their audio-visual consultant. He's also doing a little market research on the side, specifically on company towns like Hershey, Pennsylvania, though Bristow is a long way from changing its name to Berger.

On the video, shots of a town road, trucks passing. It looks like the same footage as in the Mrs. Ojibway movie. Herb Marcus' voice-over explicating that what we are about to see reveals parallels with a society in Madagascar. Cut to a diner, interviews with a waitress, Amalie's father somewhat flirtatious. He's made a hit with the locals.

Amalie still couldn't forgive her father for keeping his early life a secret from her. She remembered how he never answered her questions, always held back, made fun of her for being a nosy body. It was his own fault that she never showed him much affection. Too bad if he held it against her. There was a time when she just couldn't measure up to people's ideals. Amalie knew that. Stewart even accused her once of being indifferent to social suffering, but then he apologized, admitting he'd been wrong. And Charlie used to reproach her for being uninvolved. One doesn't have to man the barricades to be involved, she thought, switching off the video. With the exception of an incompetent boss, her job with the Task Force was just right for her.

Amalie remembered her conversation with Marshall when she told him her decision about relocating with the company.

"I know, I know," he said, raising his hands when she came in. "It's bad news. You're not coming with me—with us. You found another job."

"Not yet," Amalie said. "But I'm hopeful. And I'm sorry."

"Tell me where to send a recommendation and I'll do it," he said.

The man really was a softie, Amalie decided.

Since there would be a skeleton staff in New York, at least for a few months, Marshall invited Amalie to stay on—in a reduced capacity of course—until she found something else.

That suited her fine. It would leave her time to go job hunting. She suspected that there really wouldn't be any work for her to do at the New York office and that Marshall would have a hard time convincing Hannelore to let her stay on. But she wasn't going to worry about that.

"I'll be shuttling back and forth," Marshall said, "so we'll see each other, won't we?" He seemed so forlorn.

"You're doing a great thing, starting over up there," Amalie said encouragingly. "It's really—visionary."

"So good to hear that from you," he said, his voice breaking a little. "I have hopes, great hopes. I know Hannelore will miss you."

She smiled. "And I'll miss her of course."

Now, Amalie was helping people with their housing problems and navigating her way through the system. Not only was she paying a debt to society—they let her kid off, after all, and she was grateful—she loved the raw power of it, the ability to pull strings with a clean conscience, which was more than Evan Diaz could say, though she was indebted to him for recommending her. She was tempted to give in to his pleas to get together. It would be a novelty to go to bed with someone you know is a bastard. It could add some spice to her life. She knew that her friend Julie was dating Evan whom she'd run into at the Columbia gym. Julie had been trying to stop a defective treadmill and he caught her as she spun off it. Actually they had met years earlier, at a party Amalie and Stewart had given. "What could be more romantic," Julie told her, "though it's true that he's a couple of years younger, but so what, look at Catherine Deneuve."

The phone rang. Skip Fowler, the erstwhile barefoot lawyer with dog had taken a shine to her, after receiving her thank-you note for his brilliant work at the hearing for Charlie and his friends.

"The Vera Institute wants to hold an awards dinner for me next month. I won't go unless you come with me. I hate these things. I would rather do takeout and make-out. How's tonight?"

"I can't miss my stretch class," Amalie said. "I know you want my corpus delicti—remind me to tell you about the French porn I used to translate....No, I'm not trying to turn you on." She laughed. Just before she started her present job she was offered a position with a French ad agency with an office in New York. Their advertising copy read very much like the pornography she used to translate. "Tomorrow night?" she said. "I can't. I have a ticket to the opera and I'll be out of town through the weekend. Back on Monday evening." She was driving to Bristow, Vermont to see her father for the first time since he moved there three months earlier. And maybe she'd see Marshall who had demonstrated admirable restraint in not pressuring her to go out with him. As for Ed Fielding, he had shown his true color: puce. If Ellen, a.k.a. Endive, weren't working here as an intern, Amalie would never hear from him.

On Monday morning she was going to pick up Charlie in Bennington where he was staying with a friend who'd built himself a yurt. Then they were going to visit Bennington College where Charlie had an interview scheduled, after convincing the authorities to ignore the gym class he never made up and, more importantly, to give him credit for "life experiences." The teenage hotline he'd started was running smoothly, supervised by a board of professionals in social work, education, and medicine. He was editing the newsletter which had articles on politics, the environment, and an events calendar. In an interview on public access television, Charlie credited both his parents for instilling in him a dedication to public service.

"I'm going." Ellen Fielding looked in. "You want me for anything?" She gazed at Amalie adoringly. The girl had never been pregnant. It was a false alarm because of her gymnastics. "It messes up your period," Charlie explained at the time, relieved. Amalie said she hoped he'd have the sense to take precautions next time. Sure, he said. He'd found an herbal contraceptive in Chinatown.

"My dad's in town? He said hi."

"Hi," Amalie said without too much enthusiasm.

"My folks?" Ellen went on. "They're splitting?" Tears began to roll down her cheeks. "My mother's coming back to New York," she explained. "She can't stand it in the boondocks up there. They're always fighting."

Maybe, Amalie thought fleetingly, they're fighting about me. Not that anything ever happened. There was more activity with the guy from the Library of Congress with the highly touted incunabula which turned out to be not so great. Ellen looked like her father. Maybe that's why I hired her, Amalie thought. More likely it's because I like having another dedicated kid around. Charlie seemed to have bowed out, temporarily. He was actually looking forward to going to school. Maybe she'd have some peace of mind for a change. Charlie's last adventure was a bus trip to the Yucatan. He sent Amalie a postcard depicting a Mayan temple where human sacrifices were performed (him, a vegetarian). Two days later he was home, vanquished by turista.

> *Disguised as a faggot vendor, Romulo enters the inn. The sound of peasants making merry is heard in the background. The wedding takes place as the gypsies dance around the pole. Suddenly the lord of the manor appears with his entourage and urges them to continue. Monks take up a chant foretelling the doom of Carlo. "He is your brother," the old gypsy cries even as she stabs herself.*
>
> *When Romulo realizes what he has done, he is horrified and calls for sackcloth and ashes. The message is received on the royal barge. When the serving woman withdraws, the queen sings a lullaby to her asp. The nurse, who has been listening behind the arras, reveals herself. The boy is frozen in his bodkin. His sister, who is really his aunt, now tells him the story of his birth. He vows to find the old gypsy or die in the attempt.*
>
> *Loretta is praying in the cathedral, hoping to find solace from her debauched life. Outside, the boy is proclaimed king amid shouts from the populace. Carlo vows revenge as the curtain falls.*

Amalie likes being at the opera by herself. Listening to music and looking at art should be done alone. She didn't always appreciate Stewart's analysis of a given piece or a painting or a play. He resented the fact that she never wanted to engage in a discussion after going to an event. But opera made her want to make love as soon as they got home. All those delicious arias about repression.

During intermission she scans the audience. The usual collection of stockbrokers, courageous older women, male partners, tourists in shorts and fanny packs. Don't they have a sense of decorum? This is the Metropolitan Opera. They probably think that if they're dressed in their most slovenly outfits no one will mug them on the street. That looks like Ed Fielding in the first tier. Amalie lifts her opera glasses and stares. No doubt about it. His daughter did say he was in town. Who's that tall job next to him? Amalie recognizes the type, the kind with no hair on their arms, long legs that look good in jodhpurs, and a complexion that's had all the advantages. She looks familiar. Perhaps Amalie has seen her around the neighborhood. One of the graduate students and/or trophy wives. Ed could have called me, Amalie thinks.

The woman stands and winds a scarf around her neck. Amalie gasps. It's the same scarf as the one that was found in Stewart's car. She's sure of it. Same bold floral pattern. The woman says something to Ed and then heads out to the corridor, probably to the ladies room.

Amalie leaves her seat and quickly rushes down the stairs to the first tier area. The line for the ladies room is horrendously long, as usual, and there is the familiar discussion about taking over the men's room. The woman is considerably ahead of her. But that's the scarf all right. The bell signaling the end of the intermission is sounding. The woman turns around nervously, sees Amalie and smiles. Then ducks into a stall. When she comes out, Amalie is washing her hands. "Hi," the woman says. "Don't I know you from Columbia?"

"Not me. Maybe my husband." She's about to name Stewart but stops herself. Suppose the woman shows a sign of recognition. Does Amalie really want to know? But she can't help saying, "I know that scarf."

"Isn't it lovely? I had one like it but I lost it so I hunted all over until I found a replacement. The original was a gift."

Amalie follows the woman out and they part at the staircase. Amalie has to go up a flight. She'd like to say that the original scarf is in her possession. Even through the plastic bag where it is sealed in, it still retains the odor of Nuit de Rêve. But this woman's scent was different.

She said it was a gift. Could it have been given to her by Stewart? If he was playing around, how did he avoid being seen? Wherever you go in New York you run into people you know. Unless they went to *her* place...

Enough fantasy. Let's not make an opera out of it, Amalie thinks as she sinks into her seat. The people have triumphed. Loretta is consumed with jealousy, unaware that Romulo has blinded himself out of grief. The damned peasants, those happy folk, are still dancing. The dead mezzo-soprano raises her head from the floor to acknowledge the applause.

So many women are out alone at night, cheerfully boarding the bus, programs in hand, keys in the pocket, ready to open a door swiftly or gouge a purse snatcher in the eye if necessary. Before Stewart died, Amalie was reluctant to come home alone at night so she usually stayed home if Stewart wasn't able to accompany her. She'd missed so many events and was determined to make up for lost opportunities. Amalie keeps her money in a belt, right over her stretch marks. By the time she gets off the bus there is only a handful of passengers left, crowded toward the front near the driver, avoiding the malodorous hermaphrodite spread over three seats in the back who is being watched by the driver through his rearview mirror.

When she gets home, Amalie digs out the plastic bag containing the chiffon scarf and throws it into the trash.

Chapter 16

Hannelore has a little house in Bristow with geraniums, a fireplace, and a Doberman who is not happy. He howls every night in response to the calls of the untamed dogs that belong to the poor people living in the woods, not far from Berger MicroPubs' headquarters. They seem to be encroaching on company property.

"Those gypsies should not be allowed to live like that," Hannelore tells Marshall who is lolling on her braided rug with his strategic plan.

"What do you want me to do with them? Ship them off to a camp?"

She rubs a fist in her eye. "Why do you do this to me? If you hate me so much, why don't you fire me?"

"The company needs you." He makes a note. "Did you know that Herb is doing a study on the impact of parking lot design on interpersonal violence in the family?" If Marshall can't have the daughter, at least he's made a friend of the father. "Do me a favor and get that animal of yours to shut up."

Hannelore leads the Doberman outside. "Poor *Hund*," she croons as the dog licks her face. "You are lonesome just like me. Nobody to talk to." At least in New York there was Amalie Price. But Hannelore is glad that Amalie decided not to move up here. This way, Marshall is all hers, more or less. Hannelore decides to apologize to him for being such poor company.

"Yeah?" he doesn't look up. His shirt is unbuttoned to the waist. She would like to kneel down and bury her face in his chest.

"I'm sorry if I am edgy, Marshall. It must be the full moon."

"Have you considered a silver bullet?" He laughs to himself. She'll never catch on to American humor.

"I am going for a walk."

"Take a flashlight."

"There is nothing to see."

Alone, Marshall contemplates phoning Amalie whom he has scarcely seen since they moved even though he's in New York often enough. When she first told him that she wasn't going to Vermont, that she was job hunting, he was desolate. And when she landed the job with the Mayor's Task Force, he congratulated her unreservedly. She generously claimed that the study guide she'd worked on for Marshall on land sales in dynastic Egypt had impressed the people at the mayor's office.

Not true, of course. But it showed the kind of woman she was. Marshall thinks again, with sorrow, that he never took that hike in the woods with her. Whenever he phones she's cordial but guarded. "Come off it, Amalie," he said to her once. "You have to admit there was some electricity between us. Why don't I come over next time I'm in town. I can give you a firsthand report on your dad. I think he's sweet on Hannelore."

"Marshall, what do you do in the case of an industrial tenant who's leasing the premises—like you did downtown— but who's filing for bankruptcy. You must know about these things."

He pictures Amalie in her office overlooking City Hall Park, wheeling and dealing with developers and officials. A woman with executive potential, as he knew from the start. As far as he knows, she hasn't been at any tenant demonstrations lately. Maybe she regards them as a conflict of interest now, given her new position. He hopes she hasn't switched her allegiances. Someone has to set the example.

Marshall does believe that in her own way Amalie is doing good work. According to a recent article in the *Times* featuring the Mayor's Task force, Amalie's old building has been rescued from the wreckers even though almost everyone has moved out. Amalie Price, executive assistant to the deputy mayor who supervised housing matters, had instigated an investigation that revealed irregularities in the landlord's records. Ms. Price had discovered that the landlord failed to have the building inspected for asbestos and therefore did not obtain the necessary certification prior to the sale of the property. Consequently, the prospective buyer has called off the deal. Pending a future sale to another owner, the building is being restored to its former splendor which, said the reporter, in this case meant hot water and an elevator that worked.

Now, Marshall's hand hovers over the receiver. He doesn't want to wake her. On the other hand, she may be out with some guy. Sure, why not. Marshall misses the city with its demented night sounds. This damn bucolic quiet makes him nervous. The only sounds you hear are distant church bells chiming every hour and the barking of those wild dogs. They're going at it full voice tonight. Must be the full moon as Hannelore said. She didn't take the flashlight. Crazy beasts with all that yapping. Something has set them off. They seem to be in a frenzy.

A scratching at the door. It's Hannelore's Doberman. "What's wrong, Hunding?" The poor animal is bleeding over his eye. He can hardly stand. Didn't she take him with her? "Where is she, boy?" The dog is whining, salivating, bleeding. "What's happened? Which way? Show me." The dog refuses to move. He cowers, shivering, a look of terror in his eyes.

"Don't be surprised at my new domestic arrangement," Herb Marcus said when Amalie arrived at his house in Bristow, which wasn't easy to find. She'd taken a number of wrong turns and had been pointed "up the road a piece," each time she stopped to ask for directions. The house turned out to be a miniature Swiss chalet with an ornate balcony and a hot tub in a glass-enclosed room. It showed signs of recent use, with towels thrown over a wooden bench along with a pair of rubber thongs.

"What's different? Last I heard, you had someone coming in twice a week to sweep and warm up your prepackaged dinners." Herb Marcus looked splendid. Maybe that waitress was working overtime. Amalie was genuinely happy to see him, surprised at her own emotion. Yes, she had come primarily to see him. And if she ran into Ed or Marshall at the local general store, that would be fine. She'd ask Ed how he liked the opera.

"I had better prepare you," Herb said. "Do you remember Hannelore Links?"

"Could I forget her?"

Hannelore had had a terrible experience a couple of weeks earlier and barely escaped with her life. She had wandered into the woods and was attacked by those savage dogs. In her fright she ran and stumbled into Herbert's yard. After they sewed her up at the Rutland hospital, she refused to return to her own house. She could not be alone. "I was only too happy, *too* happy. She is an amazing girl."

A red pickup truck drove up. "Ah there you are, *Liebchen*," Herb threw open the door as Hannelore ran up the steps. Amalie scarcely recognized her in her flannel shirt and work boots. There were bare-looking spots in her crown of white hair with just a little fuzz growing. "So now I am the ugly duckling," Hannelore said cheerily. "I gave my city clothes to Najeed—you remember Najeed, no? She goes back to her country soon—there is a change in the government and she will be safe."

As Hannelore prattled on, Amalie could hardly believe that she had moved into Herbert's house. At the very beginning, just after the accident with the dogs, Herb confided when Hannelore was out of the room, he had given up his bed for her. But now, from the fond looks that passed between them at dinner, it was clear that he was back in it.

Amalie knew that Alex Dobrin had visited Herbert in Vermont with a view to possibly sharing a house with him. He must have been desperate, she thought. When she phoned Alex to ask if he was actually going to do it, he snorted. "Your father has these high-falutin ideas and besides I'm not a twenty-five-year-old female blond. I don't want to be disrespectful, he's your father after all, but he is something of a woman chaser." The next time Amalie called she was given the number of Fernmeadow Estates in Long Island. "They have me accompanying the folk dancing," Alex said when she reached him. "The food's not bad. They've taken away my belt because I told them I would rather kill myself than be among the living dead. I hear you sweet-talked the landlord into saving the building. You should move back in."

"*You* should move back in," she said.

Alex laughed. "It wouldn't be the same."

"You're right, of course." Then Amalie told him that the gargoyles on the building had been removed to avoid the risk of having bits of sculpture fall on passersby.

"How could you let them desecrate the place like that," he said. "Your husband loved those figures." As though she personally were responsible for the changes. No point telling him that the landlord refused to put money into repairing the sculptures. Alex seemed to be under the impression that she was in cahoots with the landlords, just because she hadn't turned down the chance to live in a clean, bright, functioning apartment. "I know those Title Eights or Sixes or whatever they want to tell you to confuse you. What a racket. It makes me want to write an oratorio." Good, Amalie thought. His sources of inspiration were still fresh.

"We speak in German together," Hannelore was saying. Your father is so—*wie sagt man, bescheiden*?" She turned to Herbert.

"She says I am modest." He blushed. "But of course you know I am not." He cast a lingering look at Hannelore when she excused herself to clean up. When father and daughter were alone he said, "I hope you are not shocked by this arrangement."

"My blessings, Dad." He looked so cheerful, so happy. And he wasn't criticizing her for anything. Not yet, anyway.

"Too bad it didn't work out with Alex," Amalie said.

He waved his hand. "The man has some bizarre notions, especially about music. When he came up to visit he showed me his score for a sonatina that was based on a photograph of the Secretary of State. Now, I ask you…No, he was fine as an infantryman but now he's simply a cranky old man." And you are not, I suppose, Amalie thought. "Marshall wants to see you," her father said. There is always a place for you at the company."

"I have a job, remember?" Herb still had a long way to go, keeping track of important family matters. But she no longer felt resentful. Let him be self-absorbed. He'd had a tough life.

"We have expanded tremendously," he said.

We? What a Svengali that Marshall was, luring her eminent father to this little town. She wondered if his original vision of a social experiment was being implemented. Brook Farm, New

Harmony, Oneida, he had said like a man possessed. Or was it just a medium-sized business providing employment to some local people?

"Your friend Mr. Fielding is supposed to drop by to pick up some notes from me tonight."

Amalie looked at her watch. She was staying at a motel nearby. How come Ed couldn't wait until Monday morning to pick up notes from her father? Were these people always working? That wasn't healthy. "Don't overdo it, Dad. I don't want to have to worry about you."

"Oh I never felt better. Hannelore watches over me. She scolds me when I do too much. She scolds Marshall too when she thinks he takes advantage. Not just of me, but of anyone in the company. They love her. She is angelic."

"Excuse me?" Hannelore angelic? Amalie shook her head.

Back at the motel room she found two messages on the room's answering machine. One was from Ed whose voice was slurred. Was he drinking again? He hoped they could get together soon. Yeah, maybe. She wasn't interested in being on the rebound of a messy divorce. The other message was from Marshall. "Give a guy a break for old time's sake. I'll wait to hear from you."

When Amalie awoke in the middle of the night the other side of the double bed was implacably empty. Of course it was. It always was empty even when there was a man in it who was not Stewart. She sat up, shivering. Amalie thought that grief was supposed to recede, the edge softened. But it kept hitting her at the wrong time in the wrong place. Early forsythia, a tugboat on the river, a headline on the sports page. Stewart was always there. Charlie's voice on the telephone, so like his father's. Stewart had been her only love. Nothing would ever come close, no matter how populated the other side of the bed. She just had to focus on work, lay off the scotch, get on with it.

Other people do.

"So, Marshall, how's your great American experiment?" It's mid-morning on Sunday and they're sitting in a restaurant at the local mall where the waiters move around on roller skates. There are new lines in his face and his beard is shot with grey.

"Yeah, well, we have profit-sharing and some decisions by consensus." He doesn't sound very enthusiastic. Maybe he's given up on his dream of creating a new model of enlightened commerce. "If you stay another day, I'll take you on a tour of the place. You'll recognize some of your old co-workers. Oh, but I forgot you have to get back. Still fighting for tenant rights, aren't you."

"Different venue now. I'm off the street." She looks up at the atrium, the sun pouring light onto the struggling bamboo plants in the middle of the mall. A picture of herself at work floats through her mind. Meetings, projects, decisions affecting hundreds, maybe thousands of people. The major irritant is her boss but she isn't about to complain to Marshall who might take the opportunity to suggest that she come back to work for him. Occasionally, she had thought of doing just that when the departmental politics got her down.

"I saw that piece in the *Times* about your investigation of those realtors," Marshall says. "Nice work. Maybe they'll move you up to deputy mayor."

"Not a chance." But it's not so far-fetched.

"I'll never forget how you looked on that news report when you were demonstrating at City Hall, what was it—two years ago? You were way up there for me."

Amalie bursts out laughing. "Funny you should say that. In case you don't know it, Marshall, life on a pedestal has its limitations. You could be toppled at any time."

"You'll get back into it," Marshall says—whatever "it" is. He seems almost disappointed in her. Like Alex. "Let me ask you something. What's going on with the police department in the city? You read about the cops who broke into those uptown apartments without warrants? It just makes my blood boil. Maybe I should have stayed in New York." The man is full of regrets. Is he thinking about the failure of his ambitions, all those great social schemes?

Amalie lays her hand on his arm. "We're in the country. Whatever happened to that hike you promised me? I'm not leaving till tomorrow morning when I pick up my kid in Bennington. I could do with some outdoor activity. Why don't you follow me back to the motel first so I can change my shoes."

Marshall's face lights up. "That's the best thing you could have said." Which part, she wonders, the hike, the motel, or the shoes? As they leave the food court, he says, "Remind me to tell you how you once saved by life on a bridge right here in Vermont."

"You've been reading too many folk tales, Marshall," she laughs.

As she gets into her car, Amalie reflects that maybe a long-distance dalliance would be a good thing. It will keep her unfettered and in motion, at whatever speed she chooses, free to encounter or dodge any earthly body that comes her way. Just like on the George Washington Bridge, she can be in two places at once. She feels ready for anything.

a Note about the writer

Gloria DeVidas Kirchheimer is the author of a book of short stories based on Sephardic family life, *Goodbye, Evil Eye,* and co-author (with Manfred Kirchheimer) of a nonfiction book, *We Were So Beloved: Autobiography of a German Jewish Community.* Her work has been published in print and online magazines, widely anthologized, and broadcast over National Public Radio. A writer, translator, and editor, Kirchheimer is a first-generation American and lives in New York City where she was born.

The Wessex Collective Books in Print

Good fiction does more than tell a story. It gives the gift of experience.

Sandra Shwayder Sanchez. *Stillbird.* From the strangling of a midwife perceived to be a witch in Scotland in the 1880s to thwarted love and the tragedy of incest in West Virginia during the depression thence to Denver on the eve of the sixties, accurate history is enhanced by elements of magical realism in this tale of five generations that is as ancient as the Greek tragedies and as modern as the daily news. ISBN 0-9766274-1-8 $11.00, paper

R. P. Burnham. *Envious Shadows* is a deftly crafted, engrossing contemporary novel, one of those works that is not afraid to face the grim realities of life and the cruelties of society as well as the redeeming power of love... A beautiful work that depicts life in all its grim realities, *Envious Shadows* is a rewarding read. -Mayra Calvani, *Bloomsbury Review* ISBN 0-9766274-2-6 $13.50, paper

Ita Willen. *The Gift.* Meditating upon the seasons in her garden, the author describes in poetic language and penetrating insight how the study and understanding of Buddhism helped her come to terms with the inescapable legacy of the holocaust. Touches of surrealism give this memoir the feel of a novel. ISBN 0-9766274-0-X $11.00, paper

William Davey. *The Angry Dust* tells the story of Prescott Barnes and his family leaving the dust bowl for California, but there its similarities with *The Grapes of Wrath* end. The grandson of a wealthy preacher who disinherited Prescott's father, Barnes, despite his cynical black humor, hostility to religion, and his illiteracy, possesses a fierce integrity and passions that make him larger than life at the same time he is perfectly human. ISBN 0-9766274-3-4 $24.95, hardback

Brian Backstrand's stories from rural America chronicle often small but important moments of the lives of ordinary people. Memories—healing or disruptive, constant or denied—often play an important role in the stories of *Little Bluestem* which link together rural people from various generations caught in the midst of struggle or in a moment of recognition or healing. Backstrand's intention is to lift up ordinary people from rural contexts and place them squarely before his contemporary and often urban readers. ISBN 0-9766274-4-2 $12.95, paper

R. P. Burnham, *On a Darkling Plain*: Samuel Jellerson, 56 and forced into early retirement, is walking in the woods behind the family farm in Maine one fall day when he witnesses a priest molesting a boy. From this one event all the action in the novel follows and draws a wide cross section of the town into a theme that explores the nature of evil and its antidote empathy, the force that creates community, fellow-feeling and a sense of responsibility to others. ISBN 0-9766274-5-0 $12.95, paper

Paul Johnson, *The Marble Orchard*. "...A deep, sweet story of accidental enlightenment... an optimistic coming-of-middle-age novel that will resonate loud and strong with those of us struggling to stay hopeful as we deal with aging, loss, and regrets."–Nancy Cardozo. ISBN 0-9766274-6-9 $18.95, paper

Margaret Guthrie, *The Return*. "Margaret Guthrie's poignant sequel describes the pain of families hiding the actual truth about their youthful experiences from their own children. The story illustrates how traumatic events can ruin relationships. Forgiveness and a 'spiritual' truth touches every member of the community." Minette Riordan, Ph.D., President of Scissortail Publishing. ISBN 0-9766274-7-7 $15.00, paper

Paul Johnson, *City of Kings: The Ongoing Adventures of Casey Jones*. "Like any truly gentle soul, Paul Johnson is at his best writing about mayhem, madness, mystery and murder. Welcome to Brooklyn, but look out: he's in rare form here."–Terry Bisson   ISBN: 978-0-9766274-8-7 $15.00, paper

R. P. Burnham, *The Many Change and Pass*. This novel explores the question of our duty to the earth, which entails this further question: how can we live a decent human life when every individual is part of the many who are transitory and intent upon selfish pursuits that give no thought to what remains after they pass. It begins with the mercury poisoning of a small, impoverished boy and follows Chris Andrews, a ecological activist, Myron Seavey, a progressive librarian, and a dozen other characters as they deal with the implications of this poisoning. ISBN 978-0-9766274-9-4 $18.95, paper

Sandra Shwayder Sanchez, *Three Novellas: The Last Long Walk of Noah Brown, The King and the Clockmaker, The Vast Darkness*. This collection of novellas is about journeys. In *The Last Long Walk of Noah Brown*, a young man leaves his home in Annapolis in 1965. A complete innocent, he trusts the people he encounters along the roads who give him direction until he settles in New Orleans where he eventually rescues people and animals caught in the flood. *The King and the Clockmaker* examines questions about the genesis of evil, the role of art and the nature of time. In *The Vast Darkness*, a young woman student of anthropology reflects upon the influence of isolated mountain living upon her neighbors. ISBN 978-0-9797516-0-8 $15.00, paper

William Davey, *Brother of Cloud in the Water*. Do you think you are smarter than a headhunter? Do you think you could win a battle against cannibals as well as overcome doubts from your ungrateful fellow warriors about your leadership? Do you believe in emerald winds, ruby-eyed bees, silver birds of ghosts and love without end? Brother of Cloud in the Water does. Thoughtful and creative, he encounters many of the same challenges of men everywhere. Enter the island of enchantment surrounding his tribe and discover what he really feels about justice and the world around him in his first-person narrative adventure. The story is set in 1945 on an island near New Guinea. ISBN 978-0-9797516-2-2 $24.95, hardback

Bob Sommer, *Where the Wind Blows*. In this powerful debut novel, Bob Sommer tells the story of a man who has lived with a secret for most of his life. No one has called Peter Howell by his own name since he belonged to a radical student group in the 1960s. After an act of sabotage that turned deadly, Peter escaped and blended into the American landscape. Decades later, he has been reincarnated as a full-fledged citizen and now runs a successful business and enjoys the affluence of the late 1990s with his wife and children. But his life unravels when an ambitious high school reporter uncovers his secret. ISBN 978-0-9797516-1-5

Wessex books are available from BookLink Distribution (944 Broad Street/ Camden, SC 29020/ Tele: 803-432-5169). Visit them online at the The BookLink Online Store (http://www.thebooklink.com), and under publishers choose The Wessex Collective. For further details, visit the Wessex site at www.wessexcollective.com